Ohio Reading Circle
1979   5th

Books by Christie Harris

ONCE UPON A TOTEM
ONCE MORE UPON A TOTEM
YOU HAVE TO DRAW THE LINE SOMEWHERE
WEST WITH THE WHITE CHIEFS
RAVEN'S CRY
CONFESSIONS OF A TOE-HANGER
FORBIDDEN FRONTIER
LET X BE EXCITEMENT
FIGLEAFING THROUGH HISTORY
SECRET IN THE STLALAKUM WILD
SKY MAN ON THE TOTEM POLE?
MOUSE WOMAN AND THE VANISHED PRINCESSES
MOUSE WOMAN AND THE MISCHIEF-MAKERS
MYSTERY AT THE EDGE OF TWO WORLDS

Mystery at the
Edge of Two Worlds

Mystery at the
Edge of
Two Worlds

Christie Harris
Illustrated by Lou Crockett

Atheneum   1978   New York

Library of Congress Cataloging in Publication Data
Harris, Christie.
    The mystery at the edge of two worlds.
    SUMMARY: A young girl is drawn into the mysterious
occurrences in a coastal town in Northwest Canada.
    [1. Mystery and detective stories. 2. Canada—
Fiction] I. Crockett, Lou. II. Title.
PZ7.H24123My   [Fic]   78–5326
ISBN 0–689–30631–8

Published simultaneously in Canada by
McClelland & Stewart, Ltd.
Manufactured in the United States of America by
The Book Press, Brattleboro, Vermont
First Edition

TO T. A. H.

who sailed me to Lucy Island

in the old *Topolabampo*

and also sailed the *Merlin* through this story.

ACKNOWLEDGEMENTS

The writing of this book was greatly facilitated by the cordial cooperation I received from others. I wish, in particular, to make grateful acknowledgement of the assistance given me by:

The Canada Council, who funded research in the summer of 1976.

My husband, who shared in the research, and who also sailed the *Merlin* through the book.

Capt. Ed Harris, district manager of the Canadian Coast Guard, who took us to Lucy in the *Cloo-Stung* and generally facilitated the field research.

Tom Carr, senior keeper of the Lucy Island Light Station, and his wife Vera, who were wonderfully hospitable during our stay there. They were also delightfully informative about life on the station, as their predecessors, Frank and Eleanor Glyn, had been in the days when we often sailed to Lucy Island.

Mrs. A. Leask, native historian, who knew a great

deal about her people's uses of *Laghspannah*, and the Prince Rupert historian, Dr. Geddes Large, who led me to Mrs. Leask and also showed me his superb collection of argillite carvings.

Wayne Campbell, biologist with the British Columbia Provincial Museum, who had made a survey of Lucy Island's birds earlier in the year and had much to tell me about the rhinoceros auklets.

Several members of the Canadian Department of Fisheries and the Environment. Capt. M. Gay of the Marine Services and A. Gibson of the Field Services were most helpful with information about the area. And my son Gerald, also of the Field Services, was consulted many times. In fact, it was his sailing adventures in that area as a boy and his enthusiasm, then, for the lighthouse, the marine life and the birds of Lucy Island that first gave me the idea of writing this story.

Mystery at the
Edge of Two Worlds

1

WHEN STORMS STIR THE DEEP COLD WATERS OF
the Northwest Coast and gales set the sea
smoking with blown spray, it's easy to
believe that the Great Whirlpool Maker is lurking
down there with other strange beings.

When mists shroud the dark rain forest, it's
easy to believe that the Wild Woman of the
Woods is hovering in there, waiting for children.

It's a world for ghosts, there, at the edge of the
menacing mountains where the northern coast of
British Columbia meets the southern coast of
Alaska.

But when the sun shines, the ghosts seem to vanish.

The day the most exciting and wonderful week in my whole life started, it was a sparkling green and blue world, set off by flashing white wings and white snow peaks. Sea gulls were wheeling and squealing around the ship, catching bits of bread a tourist tossed up to them.

Welcoming us to the north, I thought as I hugged myself into my new yellow windbreaker. And it seemed silly to feel a flash of fear that it was all like the gingerbread on the witch's house, luring me in to a bad end.

It was beautiful. And it all seemed so wild that I just couldn't believe there was going to be a city around the next rocky point or the next forested island. It would be a small city, I knew. But what you really expected in all that wilderness of sea and islands and trees and mountains was an old Indian village with totem poles, and with Killer Whale canoes putting out from the lonely little beaches.

Maybe my mind ran on Indian lines because Mom had taken us to the museum to see how it had been along the Northwest Coast before the white man's arrival.

"You'll love it," Mom said, linking her arm in mine. She seemed excited. Though she had grown up on the coast, loving it, she had never gone as far north as Alaska. And now she was going.

Three other teachers were meeting her at Prince Rupert, where she was leaving Joe and me with Gran. Gran had a friend with a sailboat; and he was going to take us out on a five-day cruise, if the weather let him.

I was glad for Mom, of course, but in a stingy sort of way because—well, because Mr. Dennis, our basketball coach, was one of those three teachers. And Mom was just a little too bright-eyed around him to suit me. Sure, she'd been a widow for years. But she had Joe and me, didn't she? So why did she need Mr. Dennis?

Maybe I was jealous for my dad, who had been so much fun. I was sure he was the one who had given me a crazy name like Lark, as well as my crazy height.

Being tall mightn't have been so bad if my thirteen-year-old brother hadn't been two inches shorter, or if I had been a whiz on the basketball floor and tennis court. But I never seemed to get it all together—the long arms, the long feet. And there didn't seem to be much I could do about it. Even when I slouched down, I was still gangling, the dictionary word for "awkwardly long."

"Wait till you see Lucy Island!" Mom was saying. It had been her favorite place as a child. She couldn't wait for her children to see it, she said. And I felt a bit mean thinking that she had certainly been able to wait until the trip with Mr. Dennis happened to come along, to bring up the convenient idea of taking us north to see Lucy Island and get to know our grandmother better.

Nobody had been able to talk Gran out of staying up north alone. She liked painting sea gulls hovering around fishboats, she said, and ravens looking out from the tops of old leaning totem poles in the Indian villages.

"The birds really get to you up there," she had said on her last visit to us.

At the moment, the only birds in the world seemed to be sea gulls—gliding, soaring, swooping sea gulls. Then, suddenly, we had rounded the last wooded island. And there was civilization: buildings, wharves, cars, a smell of fish, and even more sea gulls. And ravens.

And then there was Gran, with a dark pixie haircut and a rose pantsuit belted around her size ten. "Well, it's about time!" she greeted us, engulfing one after another in a hug. Time we came to see her, she meant, instead of the other way round. "Lark!" she said, holding me off for a better look. "You've grown another foot."

"Yeah, she always wanted three feet," Joe said, digging me in the ribs with his elbow. He always said something silly when anyone brought up my height. I knew it bothered him almost as much as it bothered me. And I was glad Mom started talking about the place.

She kept talking about it as we drove to Gran's.

"It's grown so much!" she kept saying. But it still didn't look like a *city* to me, with just the streets and buildings you could fit in between the sea and the mountain right behind the town.

As we slowed near Gran's place, we saw a boy walking her fence rail, a boy in cords and a windbreaker. When he saw us, he leaped down as lightly as a cat and glanced at us, as unconcerned as a cat, before he strolled off.

"Just Bert," Gran said, shrugging. "He cuts through everyone's yard."

Mom was glancing around at her old childhood home. And from the remarks, I knew she was thinking how it would look to Mr. Dennis. "I see you still have your old moss lawn, Mother, and still do your landscaping with a jackhammer." She swept a hand toward the flowers that blazed in tiny pockets of soil Gran had planted in the cracks and crannies of a huge rock outcropping in her front yard. "Or with clamshells," she went on with a nod at the place next door. It had a strip of crushed clamshell winding through pine trees from the sidewalk to the front door. A flag whipped in the sea breeze from the top of a pole rigged like a ship's mast.

"Skipper's place," Gran said.

"Skipper!" Joe sang out. Skipper Peery was the man who was going to take us out in his sailboat. And Joe was wild for the sea. He grabbed two suitcases, to get us settled in and ready.

"You don't lock your door, Mother," Mom said as we went in.

"When I have to lock my door, I'll leave town," Gran answered.

"Well . . ." Mom said, a bit anxiously. But the moment she got inside, she rushed over to the big window that faced out across the harbor where fishboats were passing. Grandad had been a fisherman. "Oh! This feels like home!" she said. "And right across there, behind that little island, is the passage to Lucy Island . . . Lucy Island." Her voice softened. "I wish I were going with you."

"Well, why don't you?" I asked. For maybe if Mom and I could get together on a beautiful little island, things would be different between us.

"You know why, dear. I've made arrangements to join that wonderful field trip. Mother! You've done wonders with the house," she said, to change the subject. "All the wood panelling and the geranium slipcovers!" Then she noticed the beautiful Indian ornaments on the mantel, the little totem sculptures that looked as if they had been carved out of black satin rock. "Your argillite! I'd forgotten how beautiful *your* argillite is! Wait till Bob sees it!"

Bob was Mr. Dennis. And *that* was really why she had taken us to the museum, I thought, and why she was so excited now. She could show him what an authority she was on the Northwest Coast

Indian art that they were going to see in Alaska. "Mother!" she said, picking up a little raven and beaver sculpture. "Have you any idea how valuable this stuff is becoming? In the museum gift shop, a carved plate no bigger than yours had a ticket for three thousand five hundred dollars. And pieces no better than these were marked seven hundred dollars and eight hundred dollars. The prices are escalating like mad. And you don't even lock your doors!"

"I've never lost anything yet, dear," Gran answered. "Though there have been some thefts," she admitted.

"You probably haven't even got them insured. And for all you know, yours may have been done by some of the great old carvers. Any good art thief would know, because even though the old artists didn't sign their work, they all seemed to have their own little quirks." She put Raven and Beaver very carefully back on the mantel.

I put my hand out to touch it. But something stopped me. A sort of awe. As if maybe the spirit of the old carver was still in the sculpture, or the spirit of the old mythical creatures.

"I . . . I like your paintings, Gran," I said, getting away from the mantel. And I really did like all the sea gulls hovering around fishboats and the ravens looking out from the tops of old leaning totem poles.

"Oh yes!" Mom said, moving about to look at

them. "But that's not one of yours," she said, stopping for a moment in front of a hazy landscape.

"That's a friend's. Down the street. Lovely, isn't it?"

"It's wonderful!" I breathed. There was something so misty about it, as if it were a painting of the Other World. And for some reason or other, I thought of Pearly Plunkl.

She was the invisible playmate I had had when I was small. She hadn't been invisible to me, though she had been a bit misty and vanishing. I had liked Pearly Plunkl a lot. *She* wouldn't have chosen me to be the Big Bad Wolf or the Giant every time, the way my friends at kindergarten did. I had explained that to my dad once, when Mom had been chewing me out about confusing reality. But Pearly Plunkl was long gone, like my dad. And suddenly, standing there in front of that painting, I had a rush of longing for both of them. I had a crazy feeling that maybe they were still out there, somewhere, in a misty *Other World*.

"What is it, Lark?"

Until Gran spoke, I hadn't realized that I was still standing there, staring at that hazy landscape. "Oh . . . uh . . . I'd like to paint," I said, blurting out the first thing that came to me and moving my hands as if I were interested in the way the lines went.

"Great! We'll go painting when you get back

from the cruise," Gran promised. "And now, what about a nice cup of tea? With something." She pried the lid off a big white plastic box and let out a whiff of butterscotch squares and chocolate brownies.

"Wow!" Joe said, hovering over the box, sniffing. "Gran, I'll skip the tea and settle for the something."

While I had tea and a chocolate brownie, my eyes kept turning toward the hazy landscape; and it gave me an uneasy feeling. Maybe there was an Other World all around us, I thought, a world of ghosts and spirits. Maybe I was hovering at the edge of two worlds.

Solidly settled into one world, Joe had about six somethings before he said, "Don't you need things from the store, Gran? Bread? Or milk or something?"

"Not a thing, Joe. But go along! You won't get lost in this town."

"I won't get lost anywhere." He grinned as he whipped out his new compass. And of course a piece of cord fell out of his pocket—the cord he used for practicing his seaman's knots.

"Famous last words," I said. "But I'll take my chances and go with you."

I wasn't as wild as Joe was about always dashing off to do things. But I had an urge to get away from that hazy landscape, and from the black carvings on the mantel. I wanted to get out into the world where the wind was whipping the flags and the sea gulls were screaming around the good, solid, smelly old fishboats. And no ghosts were hovering.

2

W E WALKED AROUND TOWN A BIT AND LOOKED at the totem poles at the museum. Then we made our way down to the sea and stood watching the fishboats go by.

"Halibut capital of the world!" Joe bragged, because Grandad had been in shares on a halibut boat. "But I guess those are salmon trawlers. Boy, would it be neat to work on a fishboat!" The very thought of it made him whip out his piece of cord and go to work on his bowline or reef knot or something.

"Well . . ." I sort of agreed. Working on a smelly fishboat was not something I really dreamed about.

But my dad had worked here on one, once, before he'd gone into Fisheries. It was how he had met Mom. He'd been earning money for his next year at university.

"Am I glad Gran has a friend with a sailboat!" Joe said, grabbing my arm to put on a half-hitch. "That'll be more fun than an outboard. Heeling over in a stiff breeze! Wow!"

"Wow!" I wailed, suddenly realizing that a sailboat *would* heel away over in a stiff breeze. I'd heard enough about this coast to know that the winds were really something. They could whip up into a gale very quickly. "I hope Skipper Peery's a good sailor."

"Phoo!" Joe dismissed any thought of danger. His mind was on the boats. "Hey! There's the RCMP launch. I wonder who the Mounties are after."

"Oh, I guess there's a lot of skullduggery out there," I said, remembering newspaper stories of dope smugglers who had cached their heroin on one of the lonely beaches. The world was pretty wild up here, once you were out of sight of the city. "You could do anything out there. And who'd see you?"

"Yeah!" Joe agreed, as if that were a bonus. "Hey! Maybe we should get back and sign on for the voyage." He stowed his cord in his pocket.

"Okay," I said. So we started walking back to Gran's.

When we got to her street, there was a woman walking about thirty yards ahead of us. And something about her made me catch my breath.

"Five foot twelve," Joe guessed. "And flagpole all the way."

"Joe!" I said, hushing him. But the woman *was* strangely flagpolish. She was tall and narrow, with a long black headscarf whipping out in the breeze. What really caught your eye, though, were her feet. At least size twelve, they moved in a flap-flap, splay-footed way, like a clock pointing at ten and two. But that wasn't what made me catch my breath, or catch it again as she raised her arms in a fluttery sort of way.

"Hey! She's going to take off," Joe predicted. "But she's going to have trouble, with those feet."

"Joe!" I shushed at him. Couldn't he see this was serious? "She's dancing like a wood nymph," I mumbled. I was really awed to see a woman do that, right out in public.

"Wood nymph?"

"I mean . . . I'll bet she feels like a wood nymph." That's what most people never seemed to understand. You could *look* like a flagpole and still *feel* like a wood nymph.

"You ought to know," Joe said, because he had once caught me dancing like that.

"Phooey!" I said, very quickly, to toss the comparison out of my mind.

Just at that moment the woman settled back into

a solid flap-flap walk and turned in at a gate a few places down from Gran's. Her yard had bits of driftwood scattered about, each one set up to draw your attention to its likeness to a seal or a crane or some sort of sea monster.

"Maybe they come to life on moonlight nights," Joe said. But I knew he was joking. Joe didn't ever believe things like that. "Wanna bet she's not a witch?"

"Sh!" I warned him. For the woman was hovering over a driftwood sea serpent as we neared her gate. Then she flapped on around the house.

"Ee-ow!"

I jumped, startled by a sound above me.

"Her cat!" Joe said in an I-told-you-so whisper.

But it wasn't a cat. It was a big black raven that settled on the roof, watching us.

"A cat in disguise," Joe suggested.

"Mom told us about the ravens up here," I reminded him. "They wake you up every morning, and sometimes they bark like a dog, or whistle. They can imitate anything."

But it was weird just the same.

"Hey, Gran!" Joe called as we went into the house. "You've got some weird neighbors."

"And one of them's here now," she called back.

"Oh . . . hi," Joe said, taken aback by the figure at the window—a man in a fisherman's navy blue sweater. His eyes were twinkling in a tanned face, and his hair was silver.

"Skipper, these are my grandchildren, Joe and Lark Doberly. Kids, Skipper Peery."

"How do you do?" I said, liking Skipper at first sight.

"Hello! So you're the crew? Hm!" he said as he shook hands with Joe. He looked pleased.

"Skipper brought over some Lucy Island abalone," Mom said. "All thawed and pounded for your first dinner on the north coast."

"Abalone!" I said, thrilled. It seemed such a right thing to happen. As if my dad had arranged it. He had told me about prying abalone off the northern reefs and had given me lovely, rainbow mother-of-pearl lined shells.

"And about my other neighbors," Gran was saying. "I think maybe you saw Winnie."

"Tall? In the house with the driftwood?" I said, trying to make her sound like any neighbor.

"That's Winnie. A perfectly nice woman. And a good painter." Gran nodded toward the hazy landscape.

"She was . . . sort of . . . dancing," I went on, to explain why Joe had called her weird.

"Why not? When something gets into her?" Gran challenged.

"Something gets into her?" I blurted out. "You mean . . . like a spirit or something?"

"Or something," Gran said, closing the subject.

"But—" I hadn't really thought before about something getting *into* you.

"I've got to go," Skipper Peery announced. "When you're taking a couple of landlubbers out on a five-day cruise . . ." He sort of twinkled at Joe and me before he went off.

Mom and Gran disappeared into the kitchen. Joe went out to do something. And I was just heading for the hazy landscape when I noticed the local paper with one of Mom's red-pencil circles around an item.

ARGILLITE SCULPTURES STOLEN

"Now she'll make Gran lock her doors," I thought. And I went over to the fireplace to have a good look at those valuable ornaments.

3

"SMALL CRAFT WARNING," JOE REPORTED NEXT
morning, right after the Marine Forecast.
I was glad I didn't have to worry about it
quite yet.

Skipper arrived midmorning. And this time he
spread out a big chart, outside on Gran's picnic
table, though the freshening sea breeze was not
really cooperating.

"Here, Joe, you anchor the corners," he said,
taking a box of pushpins out of his pocket. He
had a woolen toque on now, to match his sweater.
And I really did love the way he looked—like a
fisherman in a story, all ready to cast his net into

the sea. I liked the quick sure movement of his hands, too, as he coped with the wind.

"There's Lucy!" Mom said, putting her finger down on an island with a cluster of islets out in the middle of Chatham Sound.

"We'll make it to Lucy the first day," Skipper told us. "And here's the way we'll get there." He put his finger on the yacht club, zigzagged it down the harbor to a certain buoy; he was just moving it toward the passage, when Gran said, "Visitor coming up astern, Skipper."

We all looked round.

"Why, it's . . . Mr. Collins?" Mom said, getting up to greet him.

A thin man in a tired old raincoat was coming across the moss lawn. In spite of the sunshine, he carried an umbrella.

"Good morning, Clarence," Gran called out. "Come on over and meet the family."

"They got here in one piece, eh?" His voice sounded as if you couldn't really expect that.

"Well, in about eight pieces, if you count the luggage," Gran said. And she introduced us.

"The youngsters had to bring their sea chests," Skipper joked. "I'm taking them out on a cruise."

"Yeah!" Joe said, turning eagerly back to the chart.

But Mr. Collins wasn't what you would call gung-ho for the sea. "You wanna watch it out there, kid," he told Joe. "There's a lot of sharp mountain peaks hiding out in them waters, just not quite breaking the surface to warn you."

Actually, there were enough peaks breaking the surface to suit me. I noticed Aliford Reefs . . . Midge Rk. . . . Dawes Rks. on the chart. And you could see that even Lucy was just a high peak in an undersea ridge of mountains that ran parallel to the Coast Range. They were pale on the chart, like a ghost ridge.

Mom, too, had given a startled look at the rocks and reefs, I noticed with satisfaction. "I guess I never thought about the submerged peaks," she admitted now, with the first sign of concern for her children. "And squalls do blow up pretty fast."

"No faster than when you were a child," Gran said. "And you always got home in one piece."

"We'll keep an eye on the weather," Skipper assured everybody. "And on the charts." He moved his hand swiftly to counter a gust of wind.

"Well, just hope they got 'em all down on the charts," Mr. Collins warned. "Many's a ship hit a rock that ain't there. And even more's hit rocks that are there on the charts . . . You kids ever hear tell of the *Bristol*? Got caught in a blow out there in Chatham Sound. And struck them rocks at full speed." He poked the chart hard with a bony finger.

"Away back when," Gran countered. "And in the winter gales."

"The gales don't always wait for winter."

"That's true," Mom remembered. And again I was pleased to catch the anxious edge to her voice.

"How about a nice cup of tea?" Gran suggested, getting up to attend to it.

"Don't mind if I do," Mr. Collins said, though his mind clearly wasn't on the tea. And before she came back with it, he'd been through another shipwreck and was into the mystery of the *Mary Brown*, a sailing ship that had been driven onto the rocks at Banks Island, south of Lucy, in 1893.

"Never found no trace of even one body," Mr. Collins was saying. "Nor a stick of her cargo. Just an empty lifeboat that fetched up on a lonely Alaska beach and them few bits of rifles and watches and money the Indians turned in to the missionary when they reported the wreck."

"But that wasn't just the gales," Gran said, barging right into the story. "Don't forget they found a knife-slashed vest and coat. And there was that seaman who had signed on just before the *Mary Brown* sailed from Alaska. They found out later he'd come straight from San Quentin, where he'd been serving two years for murderous assault on O'Brien, one of the passengers on the *Mary Brown*."

"Wow!" Joe said. "You think he caused the shipwreck, Gran?"

"Well, he'd sworn to get O'Brien if it was the last thing he did. So maybe he did in O'Brien *and* the crew and sailed that lifeboat up to the lonely

Alaska beach . . . with who knows what? Winnie's great-grandfather was a mate or something on that schooner. It's why her family came here from San Francisco in the first place—to try to find out what they could about him or even track down that chest of stuff he was bringing out."

"What kind of stuff?" I asked.

"I don't think he told them, except that it was heavy and valuable. It was to be a surprise."

"Argillite sculptures are heavy and valuable," Mom burst out. She certainly had a one-track mind, I thought. "Maybe Winnie's great-grandfather went in for collecting Indian art. Lots of old sailing ships' officers did," she went on. "And those old 'wealth chests' are now worth thousands of dollars."

"More likely it was gold in that chest," Mr. Collins said. "They was always bringing out gold in them ships from Alaska. There's many a Wells Fargo safe rusting down there at the bottom of the ocean."

"From later shipwrecks," Gran protested. "During the Gold Rush. And what would a supply ship's mate be doing with a chest of gold?"

"Winnie's great-grandfather could be doing anything with anything, if he took after her," Mr. Collins pointed out. "There's a streak of something in that family. And I don't like the way that nephew of hers keeps cutting through my yard."

"Oh, don't worry about Bert," Gran told him. "He just roams around because there's never anybody home at his place."

Joe had found Banks Island rocks on the chart. "Are we going there, Skipper?"

"Not unless we get caught in a blow like the *Mary Brown*, Joe," Skipper answered. "That spot is bad news for mariners. Anyway, it's farther than I'd planned to go. Distances don't seem far on a chart. They turn out to be a lot farther on a sailboat, tacking back and forth to use the wind. And the weather's not likely to hold for more than five days."

"You'll be lucky if it holds for one day," Mr. Collins said, abandoning his undrunk tea and getting to his feet. "Well, nice talking to you folks. Hope your cruise don't get washed out. But the forecasts don't sound none too good . . . Maybe you won't be able to go," he added, with the first glimmer of hope for us. And he shambled off with his umbrella.

"Cheery type," Skipper said, when Mr. Collins had gone.

"Yes," I agreed, wondering if what he'd said about the water was going to haunt Mom in Alaska. Apparently this water was so numbingly cold that you couldn't survive in it very long. And there were no tropical islands waiting out there for shipwrecked sailors. There were no warm, palm-fringed beaches hung with coconuts and bananas waiting for her children.

"Collins doesn't know half the hazards waiting out there for us," Skipper joked. "What are we going to do if we run into the Gilginamgan?"

"The what?" we all asked.

"Oh, dwarfs who live in the sea around a certain little island."

"Lucy?" I asked.

"Well, nobody ever said it was Lucy," he admitted before he told us the story of four Indian boys who were once towed out to the island by a seal they had harpooned, and then captured by the Dwarfs who were at war with the Birds. He said "Birds!" in a terrible whisper.

"The Birds!" Mom said. "I'd forgotten about the birds on Lucy Island. Not that I ever saw them. I was always there in the daytime. In fact, I guess I wasn't sure they were there at all, in spite of the burrows. Perhaps I believed those burrows were for rabbits or something, though I never saw any rabbits either."

"Mom!" Joe said, in a very accusing voice. "You never even thought of them as being supernatural Birds' hideouts? Or supernatural Dwarfs' homes?"

"These birds . . ." I said. They sounded mysterious.

"You'll see them," Skipper assured me. "And if you think they're the birds who were at war with the dwarfs, then that'll settle the location of the war for a lot of us interested locals."

"Oh, she'll think that," Joe told him. "She'll probably SEE the dwarfs."

I ignored my brother. "I really would like to know about the birds," I urged Skipper. Perhaps they were like those terrible birds in the Hitchcock movie.

"Later," Mom said, her eyes lighting on a gray Volvo pulling up out in front. A tall man with curly brown hair was getting out. Mr. Dennis had arrived, butting in just when he wasn't wanted, as usual. I'm afraid I frowned in welcome.

"Hello, Lark!" he said heartily, when he finally got around to me. "Having a good holiday? . . . I see there's an old basketball hoop over the garage door."

"My old hoop," Mom told him. And I could see she'd forgotten all about us and the submerged peaks.

"Well, now it can be your daughter's. Lark, this is a great chance to find out you're a natural for basketball."

"I don't like basketball," I told him. And I didn't like him, either, even if the other kids thought he was the greatest thing since bubble gum.

"Just try it!" he urged me. "It's fun. And we could really use you on the team. We're a little short on height." As usual, he was being nice and hearty about my height. But why did he have to be?

"Right now I have to learn how to sail," I said, turning my back on him and pretending to be terribly interested in the chart. Which was a bit difficult, with Skipper and Joe prying out the pushpins.

"We'll make it a better session next time," Skipper promised as he rolled up the chart. And I noticed what a nice, clipped way *he* had of speaking.

"If we don't keep getting interrupted," I said, loud enough for Mr. Dennis to hear me.

"You were very rude to him, Lark," Mom said, later, when the rain had driven us indoors.

"Well . . ." I knew I'd been rude. "Why does he have to be around? Don't I see him enough at school?"

"No, you don't. You would if you were on the basketball team."

"But I'm no good at games," I pointed out.

"That's a cop out, and you know it. You'll never be any good at anything if you don't get out and try."

"But I don't enjoy games and things," I protested.

"Look!" Mom said. And the storm really broke now. "You can't go through life escaping into a dream world. Into . . . unreality. Life's for real, my girl. So you'd better face up to reality. And you'd better start right now!"

"But—"

"But nothing! Look! I've had about enough of your slouching around. So I'm giving you an order. You get out there on that boat and do things! You get out there and have some fun! Stop copping out of everything! Stop escaping into . . . Oh, you know what I mean. And it's an order."

"Okay," I said, too angry to burst into tears. "I'll go out on that boat and . . ."

But Mom didn't wait for my promise. Mr. Dennis was back, all ready to be taken out to see one of the big private collections of Northwest Coast Indian art.

"Okay," I promised myself. "I'll go out on that boat and do things if it kills me. I'll face reality." Even if reality was submerged mountain peaks and water that was too cold to survive in and birds that dived down on you and pecked your eyes out. "I won't cop out of anything," I promised myself. And I just hoped she'd be sorry.

4

B Y MIDMORNING NEXT DAY, MOM WAS GONE. RAIN was blotting out the shore across the harbor. The pitted surface of the sea seemed as heavy and dull as hammered lead. And the passing fishboats were blurred by a wet shroud.

Then the rain stopped. A breeze sprang up. The sun came out. Moving clouds raced aside to clear great patches of blue sky. And the sea gulls flashed again above sparkling blue water.

As happy as the sea gulls, Joe went off to buy a toque like Skipper's. When we'd been shopping for my blue denim sailing hat at home in Victoria, he'd said, "No way!" to any kind of a hat for him. And now, here he was buying a toque. After one visit next door, left and right had turned into port and starboard. He'd even ditched his knotting cord to carry around one of Skipper's gaskets—a short length of rope sailors used for tying up things. Joe's sea fever was raging.

He was at the boat after lunch, helping Skipper ready things for our cruise the next day, when Gran and I walked to the store for things we needed for the baking. And we were nearly home again when we heard a woman's voice call out, "Keep away from him!"

Then we saw Bert leave Winnie's yard as quietly as a cat. He leaped up onto her fence rail and down to the sidewalk, ignoring the gate. And he scarcely glanced at us, even though Gran said, "Hello Bert!"

Then I noticed Winnie standing at an easel near a driftwood sea lion. Her long black headscarf was whipping out again in the sea breeze.

"Hi, Winnie!" Gran called out.

"Maisie! I'm having trouble with that eagle again," Winnie said, flap-flapping over toward us.

"Oh? Eyes won't come out fierce enough?" Gran suggested, opening the gate.

"No. The eyes are too fierce because he says he doesn't want to sit on that snag." She pointed to a spot where I could see nothing but low bushy pine trees.

"He says?" I blurted out.

"Oh . . . Winnie, this is my granddaughter, Lark Doberly."

"How do you do?" My greeting came out without thinking because my mind really wasn't on my manners.

Winnie's didn't come out at all. Her mind was clearly on an invisible eagle. And after Pearly Plunkl, I was always interested in that kind of thing.

"You mean . . . an eagle up on a snag says he doesn't want to be painted?" I asked. "Well . . . couldn't he just fly away?" I held my breath for her answer.

Winnie looked at me. And, somehow, she was looking *through* me as she answered, "He does. Only he keeps coming back to tantalize me." She said the words slowly.

"Can I . . . see?" I asked her. And my heart was thumping.

"Of course." She led the way to the easel. And the picture made me catch my breath. It was all dark spruce trees around a bone-white snag. The snag had a few lines of an eagle perched on top, as if ready to take flight. And it was all misted over. No, not misted, because mist doesn't have an almost radiant look. Winnie was painting a vision! "Do you see all that?" I asked, in a whisper.

"When I'm able to. Not always."

"Oh, I . . . see," I said. And I kept thinking about Pearly Plunkl, and about Gran, who was taking all this invisible eagle thing in her stride. Was she just humoring Winnie, the way you do humor weird people?

Maybe Mom really was afraid I'd turn into a weirdo, I thought. Maybe that's why she and Mr. Dennis were always after me to play basketball, play tennis. But they didn't know how embarrassing it was to play when you couldn't seem to get it all together, or when you stood there in shorts with your stick legs rising up out of your barge feet.

Suddenly, Winnie looked right at me. And again it was as if she were looking *through* me. "You're going to Lucy Island," she said, in a strangely slow way.

"Yes, she is," Gran said, as if "How did you know?"

"Come on round to the studio," Winnie invited. And in her flap-flap way she led us around to a sort of lean-to with big grubby windows, where she rummaged among a pile of canvasses and finally pulled out the right one.

"That's . . . Lucy Island?" I asked, after I had caught my breath. "It's wonderful!" It seemed to be all shafts of sunlight striking down through dark, thrusting spruce trees to turn a bower of wild lily-of-the-valley and ferns and mossy logs into a sort of fairyland of green light. A strange, misty green light!

"That's Lucy Island," Gran assured me, but as

if assuring herself also.

Then I noticed the black hole leading under the roots of one of the dark spruce trees. A burrow! One of the burrows of the mysterious birds? And then I noticed the shadowy figure among the dark trees behind the glade. It was a girl, a girl in a fringed shift, with a Northwest Coast Indian canoe-hat shading her features.

"Who is she?" I whispered, when I could whisper. For she was a bit misty, like Pearly Plunkl. You could faintly see through her.

"That's Lucy," Winnie said. Her voice had turned soft and dreamy.

"Lucy? Of Lucy Island?"

"That's what she told me." Her words seemed almost eerily slow now.

"We'd better be getting home, Lark," Gran said, waving her bag of walnuts at me. "There's baking to do for the cruise."

Winnie didn't hear Gran. She was talking to the shadowy girl in the picture, in the same eerily slow way. "You told me the birds liked you, Lucy," she was saying. "So why doesn't that eagle like me?"

I held my breath to catch what the girl said, if she said something the way Pearly Plunkl had said things when I was little.

But Gran was tugging at my sleeve. "We really do have to go," she insisted. "Thank you for showing Lark the picture, Winnie."

"Lark." Suddenly she was looking straight at

me and pulling out another picture, a painting of an Indian dance mask. But she didn't say anything about it. She just looked at me again and said, "Keep your eyes open!" As if she were speaking from a trance.

I opened my mouth to ask why. But Gran tugged me along like a reluctant giraffe.

"She's a . . . startling painter," I burst out when we'd reached the sidewalk.

"I told you she was good."

"Yes, but—Does she often go to Lucy Island?"

"She hasn't been to Lucy Island," Gran answered. "Not in the flesh, anyway," she added in a joking tone. "But she's got it right, right down to the last wild lily-of-the-valley."

"You mean . . . ?" Winnie had floated out of her body? All the way over to Lucy Island? But Gran couldn't mean that. "Oh, you mean she did it all from pictures. People showed her their snapshots."

"Very likely," Gran said, as if closing the door on *that*.

But I had to know. "That girl, Gran—Lucy. I never thought of it before. But of course Lucy Island was named after some Lucy."

"And that's about as far as it goes in this town," Gran told me. "Winnie's the only one I know who seems to care."

"But I care, Gran!"

"What you'd better care about is filling that cookie can," she said, shaking the walnuts at me.

"But Gran!" I protested. "Do you think Winnie had a picture to copy? A picture of the island?" The thought of floating out of body was fascinating. "Do you think Winnie had a snapshot to copy?"

"It's possible," Gran said, once more closing the door.

Once more with no luck. "But Gran!" I persisted. "It's awfully interesting. And those paintings do look sort of . . . like a vision."

"Well, the Bible does say that some people have the gift of seeing visions, doesn't it? And *to another prophecy; to another discerning of spirits.*"

"Does it?" You had to believe the Bible. So maybe Pearly Plunkl had been a Biblical "discerning of spirits," which was an awful lot better than thinking maybe you were going to turn into a weirdo.

"Lark, Winnie's a strange woman, though a gifted one. She talks to me sometimes. And I don't make a habit of spreading what she tells me."

"But you can tell me, Gran. Please! You've just got to tell me."

Gran looked at me for a few moments, standing out there in front of her house, before she said, "Winnie told me that, sometimes, it's as if a spirit-being steps into her and takes over."

"And that's when she dances," I said. "She can't help dancing because it isn't really *her* that's dancing." It was almost terrifying.

"Yes, and that's when she seems to see the Other World, she says, right there with our world."

"That misty, bright world she paints! She SEES that!"

"Anyway, I know she's never been to Lucy. And yet that painting just is Lucy Island."

Then another thought hit me. Lucy Island was beautiful. So why had she told me, *"Keep your eyes open!"*? Was there some danger out there? Did Winnie have the gift of prophecy as well as the discerning of spirits? Had Lucy told her something?

"About Lucy, Gran . . ." I said.

"I don't know about Lucy. No one seems to know for sure who the island was named after. Someone said it was named after the first woman at the lighthouse. But someone else said it was named long before there was a lighthouse. Named by one of those old Royal Navy survey ships' captains; and they usually named places after their ship, or an officer, or an officer's lady back home in England. But someone else claimed that he'd seen in a book on place names that Lucy Island was named after a fur trader's wife."

"Can't someone find out for sure?"

"Oh, I should think so. There must be books or records down there in the archives in Victoria."

"Then I'm going to find out. It's important." It was important to find out if the real Lucy *was* a girl in a fringed shift, with a Northwest Coast canoe-hat shading her features.

"Something else that's important, my girl, is getting a can of goodies ready for the cruise. So let's get at it. Anyway, I don't think your mother wants you mooning about these things."

"She doesn't." I guess I sounded angry.

"Lark, maybe she thinks—"

"Maybe she thinks I'll turn into a weirdo? Like Winnie."

5

NEXT MORNING—FRIDAY—THE SUN HAD REALLY burst out. An omen, I hoped. And I crossed my fingers before I remembered I wasn't supposed to indulge in such superstitious nonsense. I would have liked to, though, because —judging by the craft moored at the Yacht Club— this wild, wet, north coast was not really sailing country. And the tingle along my spine was spreading into my stomach as we followed Skipper past all the big power boats.

I could see the one sailboat ahead, her mast whipping back and forth as she rolled in the wash of a fishboat that had just passed. Backed into her berth, with her bowsprit pointing out to sea, she looked as alive and ready to take off as the sea gull that was messing up her clean paint.

"Hi!" a plump young man called out from a yellow power boat tied up at the end of the float. He sounded even heartier than Mr. Dennis.

"Good morning," Skipper answered, as if he were clipping the words off with nail scissors.

"*Merlin!*" I squealed as we neared Skipper's sloop. "You've named it after King Arthur's wizard." And if I hadn't stopped thinking such things, I'd have thought that, from the way things were shaping up, maybe we could use a wizard.

"A merlin is a sea bird," Skipper pointed out as he put his gear down on the float. He stepped briskly aboard, undid a padlock, pushed back a sliding hatch cover, and lifted out the door that had closed the way into the cabin. He dropped down into the cabin to stow it.

"Now hand things aboard!" he told us. "Everything's got to be out of the way. And no skylarking while we're getting under weigh." His clipped English tones suggested that you'd better step lively on the *Merlin*. And stepping lively wasn't my best thing, with my long feet tripping over anything in their way. But I wasn't going to cop out.

"Wow!" I said, when I finally got to look down into the cabin. "Stove, sink, and everything."

"The galley," Skipper said with a sweep of his hand toward a steel sink, an icebox, a two-burner plate and the rack of dishes that ran behind them along one side of the cabin. "And you'll stow your gear in the foc's'le." He pushed aside a dark curtain behind the mast to show us a pointed cubbyhole where two converging bunks were piled neatly with life jackets and sail bags. "We'll sleep two in there, one in the cabin."

I'd probably get the cabin, I thought.

"Now, everything has to be stowed securely so it won't shift when we're at sea," he said, indicating the lockers under the seats in the cabin and in the cockpit.

"Aye, aye, sir," Joe sang out, clearly thrilled at the prospect of heeling over as we pitched ahead through giant waves.

"Aye, aye, sir," I echoed. The thought of heeling over as we pitched ahead through any kind of waves did nothing for my stomach.

"Here, Lark. You can set out the cushions in the cockpit," Skipper said, whipping flat blue vinyl pads out of the space where the cabin bunk disappeared into darkness. "Watch how they fit! And snap them down! Don't want even the cushions shifting. Then set the lifejackets handy!"

"Right," I said. But what kind of a sail were we getting set for?

It was while I was doing the cushions that I saw Bert again. This time he looked like a delivery boy, taking a box of groceries to the yellow boat. And it was while I was waiting around for my next order that I heard the plump man say to him, "But don't hang around the floats, Bert! And don't forget the chocolate cake!"

If Bert answered, I didn't hear it. He seemed to move off as silently as a cat. And he leaped along a few of the boats instead of just walking along the float all the way, like other people. Was that why the man didn't want him hanging around the floats? I wondered. He might annoy the boat owners?

"Now, if we're going to make sail, better get that sail cover off, Joe," Skipper said. "Unzip it at the mast. Undo the snaps. Fold it neatly and stow it in the foc's'le. And when you're there, pass the bags marked JIB and STAY SAIL up through the forward hatch!"

"Aye, aye, Skipper."

"Everything shipshape and navy fashion!" Skipper ordered. "As soon as you've finished with something, stow it! Nothing left lying around. And if you're not doing something, keep out of the way!"

I could see that as my job: keep out of the way or be knocked down. It wasn't that I was copping out. It was just that there wasn't all that much room on a twenty-one foot sloop—especially for a girl with big feet. And when I was keeping out of the way, I could concentrate on "learning the ropes." There were so many; and they all had different names, depending on what they were used for. There were *halyards* for hauling up the sails, *sheets* for manipulating the sails, *lines* for mooring the boat, *gaskets* for tying up things . . .

And while Skipper got the jib and stays'l and mains'l on with a little fumbling help from me, Joe rowed the dinghy around from its float and got ready to cast off.

"With the wind as it is, we can sail right out of the berth. So you can let go for'd, Joe. Then move aft and be ready to cast off on the stern line." Skipper was taking in on his sheets. The sails were beginning to draw. And the *Merlin* began to nose slowly ahead.

"Cast off! Get aboard! And keep an eye on the painter!" The *painter* was the tow rope for the dinghy.

The *Merlin* surged ahead. But not until the sails were trimmed and were doing their best did Skipper say, "Now! We're off!" As if that was the greatest thing that could happen to you.

With the wind from the sou'west, we were heeling to starboard as we flew down the harbor. And the *Merlin*, feeling the wind, was pitching gently into a light sea. She seemed to have come alive, to be surging ahead, straining to do her utmost. And everything was so quiet! Just the swish of the water along the hull and the occasional slap of the bow into the crest of a small wave.

"Wow!" said the First Mate.

I couldn't say anything. It was so unexpectedly

lovely. It was another world, a world of blue sky and blue sea and the deeper blue of mountains. It was a clean world of white sails and white clouds and flashing white sea gulls. Still, I had been warned to keep my eyes open, hadn't I? So there must be something menacing out there, somewhere.

In Skipper's world, keeping your eyes open meant watching the telltale—the wind ribbon—and the sails and the sea and the navigation spars. You kept trimming your sails to the wind so that you made as much headway as possible on the gaining tack and held your own on the losing tack as you zigzagged to where you were going.

Then we went into the passage.

"We have the right wind, with a bit of maneuvering," he said. "But among the islands and headlands, the wind shifts."

And when the wind shifted, the crew did also. You were always letting go the jib sheet, or hauling in on the jib sheet, or moving up to windward, or watching out.

"Watch out for a JIBE!" Skipper said. "The boom whipping over." And I intended to watch out, believe me. That boom was a young log. "Watch out for driftlogs and deadheads!" he said. And he didn't have to tell me twice. I did not intend to hit an almost submerged log and have it make a hole in the hull and let the water rush in and sink us. There were some kinds of reality I did not get confused about.

Relaxed at the tiller, he kept glancing aloft at his sails, around at the sea. "Keeping a lookout," he called it.

Here, in the passage, it was a green and blue world of islands and headlands, of spruce trees and cedars. It was a lovely, quiet world until the yellow power boat suddenly roared past us, churning up the water.

"Hi!" the hearty young fellow called out.

"Stinkpot!" Skipper muttered. "Be ready for his wash when it hits us! He could have slowed down."

I agreed, especially when the wash did hit us and we really rolled. So *that* was why Skipper didn't like him, I thought. He didn't have good sea manners.

"Would have been worse if one of us had been down there in the galley, Lark, ladling out soup."

"Oh no!" I wailed, just thinking about it.

Then it was quiet again. And Skipper told us about the place. Once a great winter home of the Tsimshian Indians, this passage had been lined with totem pole villages and totem-crested canoes. Now as we slipped by, I could feel the old ghosts watching us.

"In those days, Lucy Island was *Laghspannah*, the Place of Lookout," Skipper said. It was the place where scouts had kept an eye out for Haida raiders from the west, and Tlingits from Alaska.

"Place of Lookout," I echoed, remembering how it had looked on the chart—small and alone in the middle of Chatham Sound, with only the ghost ridge of mountains running under the sea, parallel to the Coast Range.

"Does any kind of skullduggery go on there now?" Joe asked Skipper.

"Oh, there are rumors now and then. Somebody moving illegal fish to a boat that can legally have them . . . somebody taking too many abalone. Whenever you're close to a border like this, things can go on, I suppose. Now, as soon as we pass Devastation Island, you'll be able to see Lucy."

"And Gran's sandwiches and cocoa, maybe?" Joe suggested.

"Good idea."

Devastation was a forested island. And when we'd left it to port, our green and blue world opened out into a sparkling blue and white world.

"That's Lucy Island."

You could see it across miles of open water. You could catch the flashes from its lighthouse.

Joe had the glasses. "The 'stinkpot's' nearly there, Skipper."

"Joe, we have to give up getting there fast for getting there with a lot more fun. Now, what about those sandwiches you mentioned?"

Getting those sandwiches out of the pitching cabin proved to be part of my "fun" as we moved out into the big swells.

"There's been a heavy blow outside," Skipper said, motioning westward beyond the Sound.

"These swells are the aftermath. And this, my friends, is sailing!"

I agreed. The swells were big, slow, smoothly undulating waves. You climbed up to a crest, then went down into the trough, then up again. A gentle roller coaster in a blue and white world. Graceful as a sea gull.

The wind began to freshen and to shift more to the west and slightly north as I staggered back into the cabin to get the cups. Skipper and Joe began to take in on the sheets. And when I got back to the cockpit, I noticed that Skipper had suddenly become more alert.

"Hold that cocoa!" he said. "I think it's going to blow in a minute." He pointed to a dark patch on the sea, moving menacingly toward us. "Put the food down on the deck! Everybody up to windward!"

I didn't hesitate. For suddenly, as the squall hit us, we heeled sharply over. There was the roll and the BANG of the Thermos, and the rush of water along the lee gunwale as it went down close to the surface of the sea. There was the noise of the wind in the rigging. Everything seemed to be straining, including me. I was leaning back, being as heavy as I could, with my feet braced against the lee seats.

As if gathering up the reins of a lively team that showed signs of bolting in a western, Skipper seemed to come extra alive and alert to take the

Merlin in hand. Glancing aloft and about, with one hand on the tiller and the other on the main sheet, ready to ease off instantly, he seemed to be exulting in the blow. "If this keeps up, we'll have to take the stays'l off. But in the meantime, Joe, stand by to ease off on your sheets!"

"Right."

But the squall passed, as suddenly as it had come. It settled down into a good, fresh, steady breeze. And I began to breathe properly again.

"Could we have capsized?" I asked.

"No. Not in that."

"But we were awfully far over."

"Oh, the *Merlin* could stand up to much more than that. We could have had our lee gunwale awash. But you have to know what to do."

"Like . . . what?" I asked.

"Oh . . . you spill the wind a bit to take the pressure off your sails by easing off on your sheets, particularly your main sheet. But you keep moving! So you're in control. So you can do things to prevent a disaster. And this, my girl, is what makes sailing fun. You're not sitting there like a lump on a log, just letting things happen to you. You're right in there, part of the forces of nature."

And that's what makes it fun? I thought. I had five days of fun to go yet. In a big, wild, lonely, ghost-haunted world where I had been warned to keep my eyes open.

6

IT TOOK US ABOUT TWO HOURS TO CROSS OVER TO
Lucy, while the lighthouse winked red at us
every five seconds. And when we met the Coast
Guard's *Cloo-Stung* coming out, we waved; and
they waved as they slowed going by us so as not to
clobber us with their wash.

The lighthouse stood on a huge rock, spanking
white with red trimmings. There was a white
bridge crossing a chasm to the grassy patch where
the keepers' two white houses were. And a boy
came out on the bridge to wave to us. He looked
about as tall as Joe, and he had red hair—very red
hair.

"Andy Fergus," Skipper told us as we waved back. "Great youngster—when his imagination doesn't run wild. He thought he had a dope smuggler on his hands last spring. But it turned out to be an absent-minded little chap searching for his specs." He chuckled, remembering. "Fortunately, Andy hadn't alerted the RCMP."

So maybe I'd have company, I thought, watching for whatever it was I was to watch for. And if his mind ran to *real* things like dope smugglers, maybe it would keep my mind off *unreal* things like ghosts and spirits.

"We have a thing going with limericks," Skipper went on. "I have one ready for him now."

"Tell us!" I begged, trying to make an interest in Andy keep me from thinking about the eerie green light and the shadowy girl in the Indian canoe-hat hovering in the dark woods.

"Well . . ." Skipper said, "it's not exactly Shakespeare. Nor even common sense. But then, Andy's not what you youngsters would call 'hung up' on common sense. He's a bright boy, though.

> "There once was a redhead called Andy
> Whose father said, 'Isn't this handy?
> If the red light goes dead,
> I can use Andy's head.
> The sailors will see it just dandy.' "

I laughed. Andy looked like being fun.
I could hardly sit still as we sailed the half mile

or so along the north shore of Lucy, close in because there were rocky islets off to starboard.
Sports fishermen were moving slowly along, trol-
ling for salmon. Just one boat seemed to be anchored. The yellow "stinkpot."

"Hi! Spending the whole weekend here?" the
owner called out.

"No. Just tomorrow!" I called back.

"Hope he stays there," Skipper muttered. "The
cove isn't big enough for him and me." He had the
jib and stays'l nearly off. Then, just as he took the
tiller back from Joe, a small runabout came roaring
out of the cove. It slowed when the man saw us.

"Hello, Rolf!" Skipper called out to the young
Indian at the helm. "Nice young fellow," he told
us, "though he does seem to tangle with the law
now and then."

"Aha!" I thought. "Here's where I start keeping
my eyes open."

"Joe, you can ready the anchor. Release it from
where it's made fast. Make sure it's properly se-
cured to its cable. See that it doesn't foul on anything. And stand clear of it as it goes over the side.
You wouldn't be the first man to go overboard
with his anchor."

Joe leaped for'd. We turned to port, slipping into
a beautiful little cove between Lucy and a wooded
islet. We kept close to the island going in, away
from the rock in the middle of the narrow channel.

"Can't see that rock at high water. But it's there,

don't forget," Skipper warned us.

"Right." Rocks were the kind of thing I'd be apt to remember. But I didn't have to think about rocks until Sunday morning. We were anchoring for two nights.

"This isn't a cove at high water," he went on, pointing to a sandbar at the far end. "The tide runs through . . . Now we're in the lee of the island, with just enough wind to take us in." Clearly, using his motor was the last resort for our Skipper. He sailed out and he sailed in.

We were moving very slowly. And as we neared the spot he had picked, he let his main sheet go free to spill the little wind we had. That brought us almost to a stop over our anchorage.

"Ready your anchor, Joe! . . . Let go!"

The anchor splashed in. The short length of chain rattled over the side, and then the rope ran out. Skipper went for'd to make sure his anchor was holding. And I tried to look busy and nautical because I saw a red head emerging from the island.

Skipper dropped back into the cockpit. "I'm going to get the mains'l off."

Joe stood by the mast, ready to man the halyards. Since the *Merlin* was gaf-rigged, there was a wooden spar up there at the top; it had to be lowered and tied along the boom.

"All right, Joe. Let your *throat* go completely, but ease the *peak* down until I can reach it."

Joe was easing the peak down. But the throat

halyard had fouled. And the sail stuck before it ran down far enough for Skipper to catch the gaf.

"Let the throat go! Let it go!"

In his hurry to obey, Joe confused his halyards. He let the peak go. And the wooden gaf came down the rest of the way with a rush, walloping Skipper on the head. Luckily it hadn't come far, and he had his thick toque on.

"What the devil!" he said, half annoyed, half amused. "I hope you're not trying to get rid of a Captain Bligh."

"That'll never happen again," Joe said, aghast.

"Better not if you want to *sail* home," Skipper said as he gathered the mains'l, ready to tie it neatly along the boom. "Hand me those gaskets, Lark."

"Oh . . . yes," I said, suddenly coming to and scrambling for the short ropes. The menace to Skipper had startled me.

"Everything shipshape and navy fashion," Skipper reminded us as he tied the furled sail.

Andy was standing there on one of the lovely little beaches, watching as we put the ladder overside and climbed down into the dinghy. Which was unexpectedly tippy.

"Careful how you move around," Skipper cautioned. He manned the oars while Joe and I settled ourselves on the stern seat. "Those swells are still with us. So, when we get near the beach, I'll let a swell lift us and pass us. Then I'll row like blazes to get you in just after it breaks, stern first. You jump out—fast!—before the drag of the receding swell grabs us, and before the next swell comes in."

"Right," I said. Edged well over and hanging on to the side, I was alert for Skipper's order.

"Jump!"

Joe, who was even more ready for the order, leaped overside with such a down thrust of his hand on the gunwhale, that I was rocked and nearly dumped out. Then, recovering, a little behind schedule, I chickened on the jump and *stepped* out. The backward surge of the dinghy caught me with one big foot still in the boat. And I went like a hippo into the numbingly cold water.

Andy grabbed me.

"Thanks," I said, weakly.

"Oh, I'm always pulling mermaids out of the water around here."

"These tails are so awkward," I said, covering the alarm that had gripped me again. Something *was* going to happen to me, here at Lucy Island. Also, I was embarrassed, as well as wet; and summer was no heat wave on the north coast.

Skipper came in behind another swell, bow first. And it had broken before he leaped out, light as a flipped dime. All hands grabbed the dinghy and pulled it up beyond reach of the surf.

"Great to be back on Lucy!" Skipper said.

Andy held up a hand to halt everything and everybody. He bowed to the mariners. He, too, had a limerick ready.

"There once was a Skipper called Peery
Who landed on Lucy all weary.
But there on the sand,
Invitation in hand,
Stood the keeper's son, noble and cheery."

He grimaced "cheery," bowed again, and then read out a menu from an invisible invitation. "Clobbered clams . . . birds' beaks on the half-shell . . . prickled sea urchins . . . and, maybe, roast beef and Yorkshire pudding."

"I'll settle for the roast beef and Yorkshire pudding," Skipper said, after a proper bow. "You can feed the prickled sea urchins to the crew—Joe and Lark Doberly."

"Hi! I've always wanted to try prickled sea urchins," I said, still covering up my uneasiness. For an instant, I saw myself as an enchanted princess caught in a sea monster's spell.

Skipper saw me as a drowned rat. "I think we'll get you some dry clothes, my girl, if you're going out to dinner. Tell Joe what you want, and I'll row him over." He wasn't giving me and my big feet the chance to dunk another outfit.

At least the dunking gave me something *real* to shiver about until I could duck behind a rock to change. And then I was busy hanging my wet things on the fantastically gnarled roots of a big, pale driftlog. Only after that did I have to face Lucy Island.

The beach was almost as pale as the driftwood, and scattered with seashells—all things that had once been surging with life, I thought. The storm outside had dumped piles of yellow-brown seaweed along the high-water mark. The tangles of northern kelp tubes were like the discarded whips of some giant sea monster, I thought, before I remembered to think that they were just tangled kelp tubes, real and smelly.

It was the woods beyond the beach that really lured me, however, in spite of the uneasiness I felt. Lucy looked as wild and unpeopled as Devastation Island, until you saw the little board ramp, leading up under a slanted spruce tree and disappearing into the darkness of the woods.

"It does look awfully dark in there," I murmured.

Only, it wasn't dark when you got in there, following the broad cross-plank walk that led to the lighthouse, somewhere at the other end. Somehow, it was strangely, eerily green. Radiantly green! There was space between the dark green spruce trees thrusting up on all sides, space for the sun to shaft down on the green mosses and green ferns and wild green lily-of-the-valley that covered everything—everything except the black holes.

The black holes were everywhere, under roots of

trees, under logs that were only long mounds holding green mosses and green ferns and wild green lily-of-the-valley. Maybe it was the blackness of the holes that made it seem as if the mosses had gathered in the sunlight and turned it into a sort of green luminescence.

"Burrows," Andy said. "The island's riddled with them."

The birds' burrows! But there wasn't a sound of birds anywhere. Instead, there was a sort of hush. Even the pounding of the surf on the north beach was muffled by the trees and the mosses, as if it were coming from another world. You found yourself whispering among the eerie, moss-shrouded graves of the dead trees.

"Hey, I'm going to hop on ahead," Joe called out. "I want to see that lighthouse."

"Watch the netting!" Andy called back. Wire netting had been laid along the walk wherever it sloped. "When it's wet, the moss gets kind of slippy," he explained. "But the Coast Guard's putting in a helicopter pad, near where you came in. And the way they haul things around is sure hard on the netting . . . The crew's gone off for the weekend."

"Yes. We passed the *Cloo-Stung*," Skipper told him. "So we have the place to ourselves—unless the yellow 'stinkpot' hangs around."

"I saw him coming back," Andy said. "And of

course a few picnickers could turn up, or a fisherman could dump his kids on the beach while he catches the big one in peace. Otherwise, it's just us and the birds."

Us and the birds and . . . Lucy? Was it the ghost of Lucy I kept seeing out of the corner of my eye? I tried to remember that there was nothing there but the shadows and the black holes. Of course, there was nothing there but the shadows and the black holes! "Are the birds sleeping down there in the burrows?" I asked.

"Maybe some young ones," Andy told me. "The rest have gone fishing."

"Not a bad idea," Skipper said. "Might try a bit of it myself tomorrow morning."

Suddenly I stopped. "Something sweet," I said, sniffing.

"*Moneses uniflora.*" Andy pointed to delicate waxen-white flowers growing on a mossy log.

"Oh," I said, strangely relieved. I hadn't really thought the sweet smell was one of those sudden ghost fragrances, but then . . .

Then we were out in the open again. The sun was brightening the red trim on the lighthouse. And the lighthouse was real and solid and spanking white against the dazzle of the sea and the blue of the distant mountains.

"Junior keeper's house," Andy said as he led us past the first white house to the one nearer the lighthouse. "Come on in and see what's squawk-ing."

"Squawking?" I asked as I followed him up the steps. Skipper had strolled along to join Joe and Andy's father on the bridge. But I saw what he meant as soon as he'd opened the door. A CB radio was in full squawk. And Mrs. Fergus was just picking up the conversation.

Andy cocked an accustomed ear. "Just some guy fishing out there. And his motor's conked out. You sure feel like the center of the world when you live on a light station."

"You mean . . . you don't feel isolated?"

Andy stared at me.

"No, I guess you don't feel isolated," I said, quickly. Though the Sound wasn't exactly sur-rounded by urban sprawl.

"Hi, Mom," he said, when she finally turned away from the CB. "This is Lark Doberly."

Mrs. Fergus was about my height and dark and pretty in pink slacks and pullover. "Lark! What a lovely name!" she said, holding out both hands. "We don't see a girl often enough on this island. It seems to run to men and birds."

"I'm so thrilled to be here," I said.

"Lark took a header getting out of the dinghy," Andy told her.

"Think nothing of it, dear. Coming ashore once in a skirt—in a storm!—the skiff I was in sank. And I had to swim for it, through some pretty panicking seaweed. It kept winding round my legs and pulling at my nylons."

"That must have been terrifying. You must have thought an octopus was after you," I said. Then a really terrifying thought hit me. Maybe Lucy Island didn't want us women. Maybe *the* Lucy wanted this for her private haunt. I put the idea away as soon as I had it. I wasn't supposed to think that way any more. "Do you happen to know who the island was named after?" I asked. I found I was asking Andy. His mother had been summoned by another squawk.

"Yeh, I do," he said. "My Aunt Effie found out for me down in Victoria. She comes here pretty often because her son's nearly my age and he really likes the island. She worked out the whole story down in the archives. I'll try to dig it out for you."

"Oh, that's wonderful!" I said, my stomach sinking. Did I really want to know that maybe there *was* a ghost hovering round?

"No hurry," I assured Andy. "Just . . . if you happen to find it."

I was following him across to where the kitchen turned into the living room when I noticed the Indian dance mask on the wall. And I stopped dead in my tracks. It was exactly like the mask in the painting Winnie had shown me. "That mask!" I said.

"Oh, that!" Andy obviously was glad I had asked. "A friend of mine, an Indian, gave it to me."

"Rolf?"

"No," he said, looking surprised. "Do you know Rolf?"

"No. But he came roaring out of the cove just before we sailed in. Skipper seemed to like him. The one he doesn't like is the plump man in the yellow power boat."

"Harry Fortune. Nobody knows much about him, I guess, except that he's from somewhere down south. I've seen him around here a lot lately." From his face, Andy wasn't any keener about Hearty Harry than Skipper. And it couldn't be because Harry had clobbered Andy with his wash. Maybe that's where I should keep my eyes open.

"What does he do?" I asked, just as if I were showing a polite interest.

"Oh, he dives a lot for abalone. But I don't think he's running a racket—though you never know." The way he narrowed his eyes made me remember about his dope smuggler who had turned out to be only an absent-minded man looking for his specs. "He told me he writes for magazines, about old shipwrecks and things."

"Shipwreck!" I said. "Hey! Maybe he's on the track of the old *Mary Brown*."

"Yeh, maybe," Andy said. "It's interesting, wondering about the people who roar in here."

"Very interesting I'm sure!" I agreed.

7

ANDY TOOK ME OUT TO SEE THE LIGHTHOUSE, which was nice and solid and mechanical, with its motors humming off there in a room where you couldn't go without earmuffs. It was so clean-swept and white that no self-respecting ghost would be caught dead in it, I thought wryly. And I loved the little bridge, with all the sea gulls squealing and swooping into the chasm to get the scraps Andy tossed down to them. Two ravens stayed aloof from the excitement, soaring silently over the rise behind Andy's house.

"When do *the* birds get back from fishing?" I asked him.

"Oh, they won't be coming in until after ten. Dusk's pretty late here in summer."

"Lark, I think we'll wait until tomorrow night to explore the birds," Skipper told me. "First night out, it's good to turn in early."

"Especially when you're going fishing at dawn," Joe added.

"Okay," I agreed. It looked as if everything was being put off until tomorrow—the birds, the Lucy story. But not the dinner. I ate a huge plate of roast beef and Yorkshire pudding and a whopping piece of lemon pie.

Then, because I had noticed it before, Andy took the Indian dance mask off the wall to show it to me. It *was* startlingly like the one Winnie had shown me in the painting.

It was an Eagle mask, with a fierce beak. And when Andy put it on and pulled strings, the beak opened. "If you'd make like a hummingbird, Mom," he said, "maybe we could have some action."

"Perhaps later," she agreed.

"You know, it's great the way the little hummingbirds tease the eagles," Andy said when he had taken the mask off. "Darting in and around that great wingspan." He ran a finger over the painted Eagle. "But I guess maybe we shouldn't do a joke dance, anyway."

"You mean . . . ?" He meant something eerie, I could tell.

"Well . . . The old Indian who gave me this takes his masks pretty seriously. This one was intended to honor the supernatural Eagle. You know—to help the Great Eagle Spirit get into the dancer."

The Indians had believed that, hadn't they? They had believed that the Great Eagle Spirit did get into the dancer, the way a spirit-being got into Winnie.

Skipper stood up. "Sorry to leave you so soon, Jenny," he told Mrs. Fergus. "But I think it's time I got Maisie's grandchildren settled in on the *Merlin*. Joe and I are going out fishing first thing. Lark, if you don't want to go, we can leave you on the beach. Can't leave you stranded out there without a dinghy, even if you do seem to have an urge to go swimming." I didn't want to go fishing. And I didn't think not going would be copping out. After all Andy was on shore. I wouldn't be alone. So I said I'd rather be dropped on the beach.

"Come for breakfast, dear," Mrs. Fergus urged.

"I'd love to," I said.

It was much darker in the woods as we walked back to the anchorage. Andy and I dawdled along behind Skipper and Joe. "At night, it's a good idea to have a blind man's stick handy," he said. "Then, if you're walking in the dark and your flashlight gives up, you can tap, tap along the edge to stay on the plank walk." It was several feet off the ground in some places.

It was only about a foot off in the spot where I

saw a yellow oilskin glove. Thinking it might be Skipper's, I jumped off to get it.

CRUMPH! I plunged through the fibrous black stuff, breaking into a burrow. "Ohhh!" I squealed, horrified. "I feel like a murderer."

"You ought to," Andy said. "Look. You can't go barging round this island like an elephant. Here, let me pull you up so you won't stomp into another burrow."

"Oh dear. I do hope I haven't killed a young one," I wailed. I felt simply awful, apart from feeling clumsy.

"Oh, likely not. That burrow may run in for twenty feet or more."

"I'll never go barging around again."

"The way Harry Fortune does," Andy snapped. So that was why *he* didn't like Hearty Harry, I thought. "Anyway, you might not get a chance to pretty soon. They're talking of making Lucy an ecological reserve."

"Oh, I do hope they do," I said.

But I couldn't forget what I had done, even though there didn't seem to be much damage. Maybe the birds liked Lucy, I thought. But they weren't going to like me any better than they liked the Gilginamgan. And who knew what they might do to retaliate? No! That's silly! I told myself. Yet I was still thinking about it when I crawled into my sleeping bag in the *Merlin's* main cabin, and I guess when I fell asleep.

WHACK!

I sat up in my bunk. Something had hit the boat, maybe the mast. But nobody else had heard it. At least there wasn't a sound from the foc's'le. So I lay down again, listening hard.

Deep, long groans were coming from the other end of the island, the ghostly, muffled groans of the fog horn: two groans and then silence; two groans and then silence. And once, between the eerie groans, I thought I heard a light splash.

Just a salmon jumping, I told myself, straining harder than ever to hear. Then I thought I heard that little splash again. Lots of salmon around here, I told myself; or why would all those boats have been out there off the north shore, fishing? I was as wide awake as I'd expected to be for breakfast. But it was dark in the cabin, with just a square of dim light from where Skipper had lifted out the door. Probably the middle of the night?

WHRRR!

I sat up for that one. It was as if something had WHURTLED across the boat. Like a rocket.

"Skipper!" I said, in barely a whisper. But there still wasn't a sound from the foc's'le.

This is silly! I told myself. You can't be afraid to just stick your nose out and see if there is something out there! I could. But I got up anyway, grabbing the sleeping bag around my shoulders. *Get out there on that boat and do things!* Mom had ordered. So I peered out. And now I could really hear the deep, sepulchral groans of the foghorn from the lighthouse. It did nothing for the charm of the occasion.

It wasn't actually *very* dark. Off toward the entrance, fog blotted out the world. But near the boat a mist-shrouded moon was giving an eerie luminescence to the wraiths of fog drifting around us. And maybe that was what gave me the courage to step up into the cockpit.

The riding light—the coal oil lantern Skipper had hauled up on the mast—had a misty halo. And Lucy was a dark loom in the fog. It was eerily beautiful and utterly lonely.

Then, out of the corner of my eye, I glimpsed *Something*. A bank of thick fog near the entrance opened for a moment; and I saw a black figure in a black canoe. It was just for an instant; but the misted moonlight caught the black sheen—as if the man had come up, wet, from the sea. And the canoe was as silent as if it, too, were supernatural. I caught my breath. Then I dared to really look. But the figure had been swallowed up by the thick fog. Had I really seen it? I turned to dart back into the cabin.

WHRRR! Something glanced off my head.

WHRRR! It passed like a black rocket. And I screamed as I tripped on the sleeping bag.

Skipper and Joe came running with a flashlight.

"What's up?"

"What happened?"

"I . . . don't know," I moaned. "Something brushed my head as it went by."

"Just brushed it?" Skipper said. "You were lucky. I never thought YOU'd go walking around at night, my girl, or I'd have warned you. That was one of the birds. A rhinoceros auklet."

"But . . . why did it hit me?" I wailed. That was what alarmed me, after plunging into that burrow.

"Can't they see?" Joe asked Skipper.

"Of course they can see. It's just that they can't maneuver. They've got short stiff wings for swimming underwater. It's why they come in like a bullet, with all that noise."

WHRRR!

A black shape WHURTLED through the mist, straight as a bullet for Lucy.

"Look, this is no place to be without a hard hat," Skipper said. "What the devil!" he went on, glancing about as always. "There's a log bearing down on us. Get the boathook, Joe!"

It was a big log, coming at us from the opening that had been a sandbar closing the anchorage off into a cove at low water. It was coming with the tidal flow and with the breeze that was sweeping out the sea mist.

"The tide's running strongly," Skipper said. "That log could have caught on our anchor rope and dragged us out onto the rock at the entrance." He grabbed the boathook from Joe and got ready to fend off the log.

Just as he had sent it on its way, there was another WHRRR! Another black shape WHURTLED straight for Lucy.

"Get below!" Skipper bellowed. And he didn't have to bellow at me twice. I was glad to get back into my bunk.

"I'll get my clothes on and stay out here for a while," Skipper told us. And I was very glad about that, too.

Then it hit me. In all the talk about the birds and the log, I'd forgotten to mention the silent black figure in the silent black canoe. Anyway, I told myself, it was just a fisherman come ashore from one of those boats anchored out there, if they were anchored out there. But I didn't really believe it. Why would someone come ashore in a fog? And why would he have a black canoe. WHY?

My answers did nothing to help me get back to sleep. I'd ask Andy about it in the morning.

No! I wouldn't. If I *was* a weirdo, seeing things that weren't really there, I certainly was not going to tell Andy about it.

WHRRR! WHACK!

A bird hit the mast. I heard a thump on the deck. Then I covered my ears with my sleeping bag. But that didn't stop my thinking. Had the bird hit ME on purpose? And the log? Even the log could have come on purpose, couldn't it? If Lucy really did not want other girls on her island . . . But that's downright silly! I told myself. This is the sort of thing

I promised I'd stop thinking. "Oh, go to sleep!" I hissed at myself. And eventually I did.

With northern summer nights so brief, pre-dawn takeoff for the rocket-winged fishermen came around three A.M. The island exploded with them.

It came a little later for Joe and Skipper, after the disturbed night. But by seven o'clock, I'd cleared out of the cabin and there was a great sizzle of bacon in the galley. Luscious whiffs were wafting out to the cockpit, where I was hugging myself warm in my yellow windbreaker.

It was lovely in the cove, with all the moving reflections in the water. The breeze had swept out the sea mist. The sun was shining. Lucy looked enticing. And glancing about, I suddenly noticed something black on the fantastically gnarled roots of the driftlog where I'd hung my unplanned washing. Something must have blown onto it, I thought. But something BLACK gave me a start.

"You know," I said to Joe, as if it was really no big deal, "I thought I caught a glimpse of a man in a canoe last night, just before the bird hit me."

"A canoe?" Joe scoffed, tying up his sneakers. "No self-respecting stinkpotter comes ashore in a canoe, does he, Skipper?"

"Not even the Indians," Skipper agreed from the cabin. "They really like to churn up the water, too. But not at night. I don't think they ever did go in

much for night paddling. And fog is pretty decep-
tive, my girl.

"Well, I just caught one glimpse," I hurried to
say.

"You would," Joe said. "Skipper, did you ever
hear of Pearly Plunkl?"

"No! And he's not going to!" I warned him.

Anyway, Skipper's mind was on fishing. "With
the dinghy, Joe, we can just mooch around the
shoreline. And if we catch a big one, we'll invite
the Fergus family for a barbecue on the beach
tonight."

It sounded perfect. A sunny day with Andy and
a lively evening on the beach with everybody
would sweep out my crazy notions the way the
breeze had swept out the sea fog. It was going to
be a wonderful day.

"That bacon sure smells good, Skipper," Joe
said, poking his nose into the cabin. He was wearing his navy toque, of course; and the end of a
gasket was hanging out of his pocket.

"Coming right up," Skipper announced. "Sorry
the toaster's not plugged in."

"Who needs toast?" Joe would have settled for
dried sea snails, if that's what Skipper had been
serving.

"No trouble putting you ashore this morning,"
Skipper told me as he handed Joe his plate of eggs
and bacon and fried bread. "There's no surf to

speak of . . . Lark, how would you like to put some of that tea into the Thermos? And wrap up a couple of leftover sandwiches."

"Anything to get you off faster," I agreed, getting set to drop down into the cabin as soon as the cook had come out. "I'm starving."

It was while I was in the cabin that Skipper called out, "Ahoy there!" to Andy. He was on the beach hunting for moonshells when I came out.

"Hi, Andy!" I hailed him.

Then I noticed the gnarled roots on the driftlog. There was nothing black there, now.

There never had been anything black there, I knew. Obviously I could see things that didn't exist even in broad daylight.

And it was like a dark patch moving on the water toward me and my wonderful day.

8

I TRIED NOT TO LET MY UNEASINESS SHOW WHEN I
finally joined Andy on the beach.

"Hi!" he said. "Souvenir of Lucy." And he
handed me a beautiful moonshell.

"I might have a lump or two as a souvenir, too,"
I said, feeling my head. "I got hit by a bird last
night."

"I thought you were going to turn in early."

"Oh, we did. But in the middle of the night, I
thought I heard something. So I went out on deck
to see."

"And there was something?" Andy asked, looking at me rather sharply.

Should I? Or shouldn't I tell him?

Get out there on that boat and do things! Mom had ordered.

"I don't . . . know," I said. "Maybe there was something." And I blurted out the whole thing—the sounds, the fog, the silent black figure in the silent black canoe. "I know I was just seeing things," I finished up, sort of lamely.

"Yeh. You were seeing Rolf's grandfather."

"You mean . . . ? There *was* someone there, Andy?"

"Uh . . . look. How good are you at keeping a secret?"

"Try me!" If he'd known what a relief it was not to be seeing things that weren't there, he'd have even made up something to tell me, if he'd had to.

He had his mouth open, as if he was about to say something. And watching, I could see he was thinking . . . should he? or shouldn't he? "Rolf's grandfather?" I prompted him.

"Well . . . he's sort of a strange old man. I guess he came from a long line of medicine men or something, and now that he's old . . . well . . ."

"I'll never breathe a word of it to anyone." I crossed my heart.

"Well . . . Rolf kind of indulges him, I guess. You know the way Indians are with their old people. He brings him out here sometimes to camp, though I've never pried into just *where*.

And he brings that little Fiberglas canoe with him.
I don't think the old man really goes for Fiberglas. But it's light enough for him to handle when
he wants to stow it somewhere out of sight. He's
quite an artist, I guess. Makes masks and things.
And he's painted that canoe black and put a
really neat totem on it. Black, too, outlined in
white."

"But why black?"

"My guess is that he's got a thing about the
birds. The canoe's totem does make you think of
a rhinoceros auklet. And the old man does seem
to move around at night, like the birds."

"I know," I said. "I was petrified. I thought I
was seeing things. You know what, Andy?" I went
on. "I even thought I saw something black this
morning, hanging on those drift roots."

Andy scowled at me before he said, "You did. That black rag was a message." He patted a pocket. "Means he wants Rolf to come out for him Sunday evening. I'll send the message, sort of coded, on the CB . . ."

"I'll never breathe a word," I promised.

"You'd better not. If rumors got out, we'd have people prying round, spoiling things for the old man. As it is, I'm afraid that guy in the yellow boat is going to run into something—if he doesn't drown the old man first, roaring past him in the dark . . . Look. We'd better get up there for breakfast."

"I'm starving," I agreed, heading for the ramp.

It was beautiful in the woods, with the morning sun shafting down on the green mosses and green ferns and wild green lily-of-the-valley. Even the holes didn't seem so black in this light.

"Those birds really do whurtle in!" I said.

"You'd better believe it!" Andy said, stopping to impress it on me. "One knocked a guy off a driftlog last spring. Another had his glasses broken."

I wondered what *they* had done to annoy the birds. But I didn't mention it. No need to let Andy know that I did have some pretty weird ideas, even if last night's hadn't been one of them.

"And it's not too smart to touch them—if you ever get the chance. Those beaks grab on like a crab's pincers. I know. I once had to get my Dad to pry one off me with a chisel."

"So they're really lethal . . . Maybe they *were* the birds that were at war with the dwarfs," I blurted out before I thought.

"The what?"

I told him Skipper's story of the Gilginamgan as we walked on along the plank walk. "Of course nobody *says* it was Lucy," I quoted.

"It was Lucy," Andy decided. "So I'll keep an eye out for the dwarfs." I could see that he liked the idea. "Here we are. I hope Mom has the griddle hot. We're going to have blueberry pancakes."

I loved having breakfast on the light station, with the big ships passing in the distance and the small power boats moving closer to Lucy. Even the squawking on the CB made it all feel so different.

Mr. Fergus didn't ever seem to go on the CB. He had another radio where he sent in weather reports. Also, he was a ham radio operator. And I could see what Andy meant. You really did begin to feel as if you were the center of the world.

I didn't listen *too* hard when Andy sent out a very peculiar message. To Rolf, I felt sure. And I offered to help wash up after breakfast.

"No, thank you, dear," Mrs. Fergus said. "You go out and explore the island."

I rather wondered how you could explore the island without plunging into burrows and feeling like a murderer. But Andy knew a good trail down to the north beach; and he didn't know that my clumsiness wasn't all from not being used to the trail.

Then we scrambled over rocks and hung over the tidal pools. "I love all these things that grow in tidal pools," I told Andy, remembering how my dad had taken us to watch them.

"You ought to see it out on an abalone reef!" he told me. "You see all those great silvers and purples—*laminarians* and *red sea laver* and *purple sea star* and *irridescent kelp*, all moving with the swells."

"I'd love to see it," I said.

"As long as you don't clean out the abalone," Andy answered. "You know, the abalone used to be pretty safe when the Indians and the old-timers could take them just at the minus tide—when the water's low enough to bare those rosy-purple places where they're muscled onto the rocks. But now, divers go down at any tide. And they could really clean them out, or even just take so many that the starfish move in, or the sea urchins, and put the abalone out of business."

"But that would be terrible!" I burst out. "Do you think Harry might be doing that?"

"I don't know." He always frowned when you mentioned Harry.

"But isn't there a Fisheries patrol? Don't they have limits?"

"Sure they have limits. But divers can sneak a load of abalone ashore and sell it on the quiet.

Especially around a border. You know we're just about on the border, don't you? That's Alaska over there." He pointed to the distant blue mountains.

"Alaska! That's where Mom is, with some other teachers." It occurred to me that I hadn't thought all that much about Mom since I'd come to Lucy Island. "But do you think Harry could be an abalone poacher?" I asked, mainly to bring the conversation back to what might be going on around Lucy Island.

"I don't know. He's always zooming into town with a sack of abalone dragging in the water—to keep it fresh. But maybe they're just gifts to the old-timers who show him their native art collections. He's very interested in Indian art. When he came up to the house once, he sure looked over that mask of mine."

"That mask," I said, wanting to bring even that back to real things. "Was it Rolf's grandfather who gave it to you?"

"Yes. You know how Indians are. If you do something for them, they do something for you. I take messages and leave water on the beach for the old man. So he gave me the mask."

Should I? Or shouldn't I tell him about the mask?

You get out there on that boat and do things!

"Look Andy. I looked at that mask again this morning. And I know I saw a painting of it." I told him about Winnie's paintings, though I didn't mention the ghost in the woods. I didn't want him to know that *that* was why I was so interested in Lucy of Lucy Island.

"I wonder where she saw the mask," Andy said. He was really interested.

"Maybe in your house, in a vision or something," I said, as if *some* people believed in crazy things like that.

"Oh sure!" he said, as if he certainly was not one of the people who believed in crazy things like that. "I wonder where the old man got it. I just assumed that he'd made it. But Harry did talk as if it was an old mask."

I took a deep breath and plunged in. "Maybe it was something from the chest Winnie's great-grandfather had on the *Mary Brown*," I suggested.

"The what?"

"You've heard of the *Mary Brown*."

"Everybody has. But I've never heard of any chest . . . Hey! That ship was wrecked down there on Banks Island, not all that far from where Rolf and his grandfather live."

"So!" I told him what Gran had said about the old chest, and what Mom had suggested.

"Look!" Andy said. "If there *was* a chest of argillite and masks and things, and if Rolf's family kept it, there's nothing wrong in that. By the old native law, anything that washed up on your beach was yours. And I guess maybe that's the salvage law now, too. I'd bank my life on Rolf's honesty, and his grandfather's."

"But . . . Skipper did say something about Rolf getting into trouble with the law," I pointed out.

"Sure. Lots of Indians do. And it isn't always exactly their fault . . . Hey!"

"Hey what?"

"Look. If you could be suspicious of them, maybe other people could be, too. What if Harry is a cop? A plain-clothes Mountie or something? And what if *he* thinks he's on to something? You know there've been some thefts of Indian stuff lately. I've heard guys talking on the CB. And Harry does go around being very interested in art. He could be finding out things."

"Wow!" I said. "Look, Andy. You don't think the old man could be hiding something on one of the islets, do you?"

"Of course not. But maybe Harry does. He sure puts on that wet suit a lot and goes mooching around the shoreline. I just thought he was noting the marine flora and fauna for his magazine pieces."

"It's a good cover," I pointed out.

"If the old man is hiding anything, I think it's a dancing blanket and a dance mask or something. I think he's into spirit power. Maybe he shakes rattles and does dances."

"But what for?"

"Who knows? It could be to put a hex on those

supertankers they're threatening to run along this coast. Oil spills could really wreck it, you know. Hey! Lucy would be the place for that, wouldn't it? It's a real lookout on the Alaska shipping lanes."

"They used to call it *Laghspannah*, the Place of Lookout."

"You really do know a lot about this place," Andy said. "But no," he went on. "This is crazy. Here we are, working up a whole criminal case on a weirdo woman who saw an old dance mask in a vision or something."

"Really crazy!" I agreed. And I thought of the case he'd worked up from watching an absent-minded little man searching for his lost specs. "And anyway, Hearty Harry can't be an under-cover Mountie or he'd never zoom around the way he does, not caring about the rules of the sea."

"Why not? It's a good cover. Like his writing. Like being an art collector . . . Hey, look!" The yellow boat was anchored out there again, and Harry was just diving in, in his wet suit.

"You've just talked me back into the case, Andy," I told him. "And has it occurred to you that those things are also a good cover for a thief? What if Rolf's grandfather *has* got a valu-able old chest of Indian art stashed away on one of the islets? And what if Harry's a thief who's got wind of it?"

"Hey! Yes!" Andy said.

"But wait a minute!" I cautioned. "I don't think that family would have kept a chest from the *Mary Brown*. Gran mentioned the rifles and watches and money the Indians found. They turned them in to the missionary when they reported the shipwreck."

"Rifles and watches and money, sure," Andy countered. "But what Indian would turn in 'heathen' sculptures and dance masks to a missionary who had probably already burned the old 'heathen' totem poles?"

"Wow!" I said. "Then I really do think we're on to something. I'm betting the Indians have the old art stashed away around here, and a thief is after it."

"If I thought that, I'd alert the RCMP to protect it," Andy said. "But I'm not sure I think that. There *have* been art thefts lately. Rolf *has* been in trouble with the law. Harry *could* be a Mountie. And I'm not informing on my friends." He looked very unhappy about the whole thing.

9

WE WERE ON THE BEACH BY THE ANCHORAGE because we'd seen Harry surface near that shore just after a green boat had putt-putted in. There was a man and a woman on board it, with a dog, a yappy little terrier.

"You're sure you can keep your mouth shut?" Andy whispered. "Even around Joe?"

"Especially around Joe," I whispered back. "He already thinks I imagine things." I almost told him about Pearly Plunkl. But why should I? It was so pleasant to have someone think I was sensible. So, instead, I started being interested in a sea gull.

"You ought to see the birds here in spring!"

Andy said. "Especially the mothers! Last spring one mother swallow kept flying around Mom's legs every time she went out—to make her stop and admire the baby swallows. And I watched a mother sea gull keep belting her young one off a driftlog, to make him fly."

"The sea gull sounds more like my mom," I said, wishing she had been more like the mother swallow.

"Mine, too," Andy said. "Mom's belting me off the island for this next school year, though there's nothing wrong with the government correspondence school that I can see. I'm going to stay at my aunt's place."

"In Victoria!" I exclaimed. Then it hit me that Andy was going to see me towering over all those neat little girls with size nothing feet that didn't trip over a shadow. I wished I could stay at Lucy forever. Unless . . . unless there really was a ghost here. "You didn't happen to find the Lucy story?" I asked, very casually.

"Mom thinks she knows where it is. She'll try to dig it out later."

"Oh, just if she has time," I protested.

The green boat was anchored now. And it looked as if the man and woman were getting ready to bring their dog ashore in the dinghy.

"Strangers," Andy whispered.

"Hi there!" Harry called out to them. "Sorry! But I'm a Friend of the Birds. And I have to ask you not to bring your dog ashore. The island's full of young birds down in their burrows. In fact, it's being made into an ecological reserve to protect them. Sorry!"

"Oh dear!" the woman said. "And Skeek so wanted a run!" She turned to her husband. "Maybe we'd better go somewhere else, Eric."

Eric scowled at her, then at Harry. But he began to pull up the anchor.

Harry dived in and made for the entrance.

"Well, that's a new one!" Andy told me. "Harry's no Friend of the Birds. He doesn't give a hoot about the young ones down in the burrows, or why would he go barging around like an elephant himself?"

"Then why didn't he want the dog on shore?" I wondered.

"Yeh! Why? Why didn't he want a little terrier sniffing around, digging up things?"

"Andy! He's no Mountie. He's up to something himself." I just knew it.

"Well . . . Keep your eyes open!"

It was like an echo of Winnie's warning to me. And I guess my mouth dropped open.

"Now what?" Andy asked me.

"Andy! When Winnie was showing me the painting of the mask, she looked at me in a peculiar way and said, '*Keep your eyes open!*'"

"Your eyes open. And your mouth shut," Andy agreed.

"Oh! I just thought of something else. When we were sailing in, Harry asked us if we were spending the whole weekend here."

"And did you tell him?"

"Yes, I did," I said, realizing that maybe I should have kept my mouth shut a little sooner.

"So he knows you're going to be away by tomorrow," Andy said, narrowing his eyes. "He knows the fishermen go home Sunday evening. He knows the Coast Guard crew doesn't come back till Monday morning. And for all I know, maybe he's caught on to my CB code and knows the old man is going out, too. If he knows about the old man. Which I hope he doesn't."

"Wow!" I said.

"Well, it's a long time until tomorrow night. So come on, and I'll show you the midden."

"Midden?"

"You know. An old clamshell dump from a time when there was an Indian camp here." He nodded toward the Passage where the Indians had had their winter villages. "They used to come here for sea lettuce and sea gull eggs and abalone. You can't get abalone in there at Metlakatla. It has to be out on exposed rock in deep sea."

He led the way along the walk to where it had been cut through the midden. There was a straight wall of black earth and clamshell. And the clamshell looked old and ghost-white there in the shadows.

"They pretty well had to camp *here*," he told me. "The only place on the island where they could get water." He guided me carefully behind the midden and the big tree growing out of it to show me some skunk cabbages.

"*Lysichitum americanum.* Sure sign of water. See. There's a sort of stream running."

"Well . . ." It was wet around there, with maybe a tiny ripple of movement among the greenish-yellow hoods. "But isn't there water around your house?" I asked. "Haven't you got a well or something?"

"We use rainwater. We have a system for collecting it off the roof."

"Off the roof? . . . But I guess the roof is clean here," I rushed to say, to gloss over what might have sounded like being finicky about a perfectly good old water supply. "You haven't much industrial pollution around here."

"No. Just the birds to muck up the roof."

"The birds? Do the rhinoceros auklets roost on your house?"

"No, or we'd sure be in trouble. A museum bird man was here earlier on. And he estimated fifteen thousand pairs. They're breeding everywhere except on that one islet to the southwest. But with their webbed feet, they can't roost any better than a duck."

"So the sea gulls are your problem."

"Not any more." I noticed he flushed a little.

"Why? . . . Not any more?" I asked, though I had a vague feeling that I didn't really want to know.

"Look, if I tell you something, Lark, you won't go blabbing it round?"

"Of course not."

"Well . . . when we first came here, the sea gulls were always up there, contaminating our water supply. And . . ."

"But that must always happen on a light station," I said, to keep a reluctant conversation going. "You never see a picture of a lighthouse without a few sea gulls flying round."

"Yeh. And a lot of the keepers shoot at them. You know . . . to make the roof an unpopular roost. Anyway . . ."

"Anyway . . ." I prompted him, though I was still vaguely uneasy about what he was going to tell me.

"Well. Dad won't shoot at birds. And he's talked a lot to the old Indian, I guess, about . . . you know . . . the 'good old days.' If an Indian had a problem in the good old days—like having to catch a seal or something—he talked to the Great Seal Spirit or the Great Salmon Spirit, or whatever, and got a little cooperation." He was really flushing now.

"Tell me!" I begged him; and I found I was speaking in a whisper.

"Well . . . we had this problem with the sea

gulls contaminating the water supply, and Dad sure wasn't going to shoot at them. So . . ."

"So?" I insisted.

"So I guess he thought he'd give the old Indian idea a whirl. Anyway, every night before he went to sleep, he concentrated on the sea gulls' Chief or whatever. Sort of said, 'Look! It's nice for you up there on our roof. But you're contaminating our water supply. So how about lighting somewhere else?' "

"And what happened?"

"Well . . . You sure are persistent."

"I'm just terribly interested."

"Well, one day, after about a month of this, two big sea gulls chased the others off the roof. They did it several times. And then the sea gulls stayed off. But—"

"You're not going to say it was just a coincidence!"

"No. But Mom says, 'Phooey!' She says *she* had started feeding the gulls off the bridge every night at six o'clock. She says *she* made the rock and the bridge popular. And anyway, Dad's a great kidder. Maybe he didn't do it at all."

"But he says he did."

"Just to us, one night when we were joking about all the birds here. And we sure haven't mentioned it on the CB. We haven't sent the idea in to the anti-contamination people, either. I guess maybe he didn't really do it."

"But maybe he did!" Maybe he *had* talked to the Great Sea Gull Spirit; and the sea gulls *had* cooperated. It was easy to believe that on Lucy Island.

"I shouldn't even have told you such a silly thing. Dad sure wouldn't want it blabbed round. You know, lots of light keepers do go off their rocker from the isolation."

"But you said—"

"I said *we* don't feel isolated, because we go right along with the lighthouse situation."

"The way Skipper goes along with the wind," I said, to show I understood. "He positively loves cooperating with the forces of nature, no matter how squally they are. Andy, maybe that's what your father was doing. Just cooperating with the forces of nature. The spirit forces."

"Phoo! He was just kidding." Clearly Andy didn't like the whole idea of spirits. He had just plunged into something he hadn't been able to get out of.

"Your father has to be a terribly sensible man to be in charge of a light station," I said, to show him I understood that, too.

"Well, don't think he isn't!" He almost snapped it at me.

"But—" But that wasn't what I'd meant at all. I'd just meant that if such a sensible man did think there was something to this spirit thing, then maybe there was. Why shouldn't there be nature spirits? Right now, though, I was sensible enough to trim my sails to the wind that was blowing. "So now we've each told each other a crazy little story about Lucy Island," I said.

"Yeh. But some stories are not for telling."

"Right. And wild killer whales couldn't drag your story out of me. Did you say the Coast Guard's putting in a helicopter pad?" I asked, just to show how completely I had wiped nature spirits from my mind.

"I'll show it to you. Come on!"

We walked back down the plank walk, through the woods. And when the walk branched two ways, we followed the one to the right, to a spot where it cut through thick clumps of salmonberry bushes.

"This must have been terrible for the birds," I said, looking at the flat, blasted-out square overlooking the anchorage.

"Asphyxiated a lot of them, I guess. And for a while there, they were hitting the house all night and clobbering themselves on the tower. The Coast Guard's work's pretty important, and you have to weigh one thing against another. But when all that chopping and blasting started, I guess a lot of the birds said, 'There goes the neighborhood!'"

I laughed. "At least the helicopter's likely to come in the daytime, when the birds aren't around," I pointed out. "Skipper said we could explore the birds tonight. But what are they like?"

"Oh, you'll see."

While we were standing there, I saw Joe come out of the *Merlin's* cabin. So I shouted to him.

"Hi!" he called back. Then he yelled "LOOK!" and held up a big silver salmon.

"So the beach barbecue's on," I said.

I was back on a gaining tack. Nothing eerie could happen at a beach party.

10

"DID YOU SEE THE BARBECUE PLACE?" ANDY
asked as we headed for the beach.

"No."

"Well, come on!"

Actually, it wasn't far from the ramp. But it
was lost in the rocks behind the gnarled roots
where I had hung my wet clothes. People from
the mainland had made it right in the rocks, using
cement to hold the grating and to make a hole at
the back to let the smoke out.

"Since Skipper and Joe caught the fish, maybe
you and I can get the firewood ready," Andy said.
"I'll get an axe and saw. And I'll tell Mom the

Ferguses are eating out. Lucky the junior keeper's on duty tonight, because Dad plays a great banjo for singing."

"Great!" I said. And I sat down on a driftlog and hugged myself. Mom had been right about one thing. I had needed to get out and have some fun. So maybe she was right about other things, too. As of this minute, I'd forget about nature spirits and ghosts. I'd think that Winnie *had* seen pictures of Lucy Island; that Mr. Fergus *had* been kidding about the sea gulls; and that Lucy *would* turn out to have been an officer's lady back home in England.

When Andy came back, we got the firewood ready.

"Remember to tell Skipper that Mom's bringing a salad and hot rolls, as well as the cups and things," he said, when Joe started rowing ashore to get me. The fire was laid, ready for the match. And the guests weren't going to turn up until nearly seven. "After Mom's fed the sea gulls," Andy reminded me. "Got to keep them off the roof."

"I should say so!" I agreed.

The *Merlin's* facilities weren't the greatest; but I thought I looked rather nice when I checked in Skipper's shaving mirror about six o'clock.

The salmon looked gorgeous. Skipper had cleaned it and cut it into flat steaks—thick, salmon-pink steaks with one silver surface.

"Ever had salmon barbecued on a beach?" he asked me.

"No. I've gone in more for hot dogs."

"Well, you wait! With the salad and hot rolls Jenny's bringing, it'll be a feast for a chief."

"And we are going to see the birds tonight?" I reminded him.

"Soon as it's dark enough. Right now, we'd better go ashore and get that fire going."

We rowed ashore. And soon the blue wood-smoke was curling up from the rocks; Skipper was brushing the salmon with his special mixture; and my mouth was watering.

"We won't put it on till they get here," he said. "It doesn't take long."

The fire was all hot coals by the time we heard the mini-tractor rumbling along the plank walk. And when Joe and I darted over to help carry things, we found they had brought backrest seats and rugs as well as a beautiful salad tossed up in one wooden bowl and a pile of crusty rolls in another.

"Wow!" Joe said. "This is going to be a barbecue!"

It was. I had always loved fish. But I'd never tasted any as delicious as that barbecued salmon. I thought I'd never eat again, I was so full.

It was when Mr. Fergus started to strum a bit on his banjo, between chats with Skipper, that I suddenly wished there were public washrooms on the island. But there weren't. So I waited until Andy went off to show Joe the helicopter pad before I looked about for a place to go.

Anywhere along the plank walk was out, with those burrows tunneled everywhere. And how did I know where the boys would get to? They might drop down to the beach and turn up anywhere.

The islet seemed the likeliest place for a lady in distress. So I said to Mrs. Fergus, "I'll be back in a few minutes."

"Fine, dear." She was rinsing the plates off in the sea. "Run up to the house if you like."

"Oh no, thank you," I said. The house was half a mile away, through those shadowy woods. And anyway, I might run into the boys.

I happened to glance south, where peeps were skimming across the water with their thin, scraping little cries. The kelp that had gathered into rafts away out at sea was shimmering in the late sun. And maybe it was that brightness that made the connecting rock look so black when I glanced back toward the islet.

It was a water-smoothed ridge of black rock joining the islet to the island at low water, yet standing like a low barrier between them. And you couldn't go round it because both ends ran down into water. Still, it looked easy enough. Until I started across it. Then I kept slipping and slithering on the marine growth; and there didn't seem to be any toeholds.

If I hadn't eliminated my crazy imagination, I'd have thought that black ridge was trying to keep me from going over to the islet. But when that thought did strike me, I got rid of it fast by reminding myself that there was nothing strange about *me* being awkward on slippy, uneven rock. Anyway, I'd sworn to do things. And besides, right now I needed to.

I made it over to the shingly beach. And the trees that came right down to the long coarse beach grasses had such a jungle of undergrowth that I had to push branches aside to get in out of sight.

I found myself in a little clearing. The trees had been just a fringe. I did not plan to linger one moment longer than I had to. That clearing was a spooky place. It seemed to have a green sheen; yet there was no grass or moss on the fibrous black earth. Just spruce needles and cones. And then I saw the HOLE. An enormous black hole! Like a cave. Or an animal's den. Or the burrow of the Great Rhinoceros Auklet Spirit himself.

Sometime or other, a big tree had toppled over, and its towering roots had taken great clods of the forest floor with them, leaving a gigantic hole. But this hole was more than that. It was as if a thousand rhinoceros auklets, working together, had dug a burrow. Or as if the Gilginamgan's enemy birds had carved out a hiding place.

Glancing nervously about, I didn't see any smaller black holes. And I remembered that Andy had said the birds were breeding everywhere *except on that one islet to the southwest.* This was the islet to the southwest. And there had to be some reason why the birds didn't breed here. Some unnatural reason?

I kept holding my breath. It was all so silent . . . so waiting . . . With the dim, eerie green light. Not a lovely, sun-shafted fairyland world like Lucy Island. There was something darkly menacing here. I felt a presence, silent and waiting. And I couldn't seem to move.

I caught my breath when I saw the opening in the jungle of forest behind the clearing. It was to the left of the towering roots and the hole; and it led to another, smaller clearing, with more dark, gloomy forest behind that.

Several low, ghostly moans came from that forest.

Then there was silence again. That terrible, waiting, menacing silence.

Then I caught a movement, away back there in the gloomy forest behind the other clearing. Something black moved in the almost-blackness of the forest. And I held my breath, as terrified as if I had stumbled into some forbidden world a million miles from nowhere. The thing seemed to be black and wide, more like a giant bird than like a man.

And I sensed—if I didn't see—the hardness of a bird's beak and the glittering brightness of a bird's eyes.

The Great Rhinoceros Auklet Spirit! The Spirit that had seen me plunge into the sleeping burrow . . . the Spirit that had whurtled the bird at me in the middle of the night . . . the Spirit that was waiting now for something further that would happen to me.

The sudden roar of a low plane broke the awful spell. And I fled from the terrifying presence.

Somehow, I got back across the black rock, slipping and picking myself up.

"What is it, dear?" Mrs. Fergus asked me. "You're not sick?" She was a nurse, I knew.

"Oh no. I just . . . slipped on the rocks." The knees of my blue jeans backed up that story. "I'm awfully clumsy."

"Nonsense. Sea rocks are tricky when you're not used to them. Look, dear. The kettle's on. What if I made another pot of tea?"

"Oh yes, please!"

"Won't be a minute. You just sit there." She led me to a backrest and threw a tartan rug around my shoulders.

How could I have been so terrified? I thought. There, on that islet, a stone's throw from all these warm, friendly people on the beach! Why was I such a scary person? Why did I have these hallucinations? There couldn't have been anything on that islet.

Or could there? Was Mom wrong about reality?

Mr. Fergus was strumming away and I had a nice hot mug of tea in my hands when the boys came back.

"Sorry we were so long," Andy said, coming straight to me. "But I remembered I'd left that Lucy story on the dresser. So we went to get it." He held up a big manila envelope. "Take it with you tomorrow . . . Hey! Is something the matter?"

"Oh, I . . . slipped on some rocks and bruised myself a bit. Would you just put that on the log for now?" I didn't want to touch it, because I was afraid of what it might tell me.

"Dad!" Andy said. "How about 'Dress me up in me oilskins and jumper'? I really like those old sea songs."

"Me, too!" I said.

"If you'll all sing along," Mr. Fergus agreed, strumming into the sea song.

"Where are you heading for tomorrow, Skipper?" he asked, when the song was over.

"Haven't quite decided yet. So many good places to go for a day's sail. I'm torn between the Melville Group and Squaderee. I like that rolling muskeg down there, with the low pines."

"Nice beaches down that way, too. But you won't find a nicer spot than Lucy. There's something about this island. A sort of benevolence. I guess there's a good Spirit hovering over Lucy."

"Dad and his spirits!" Andy said, as if it were a family joke. "You'd better watch it, Dad, or people are going to think you mean it."

Mr. Fergus laughed as if it were all a joke. But he had said "Spirit." And maybe he hadn't been kidding about the Great Sea Gull Spirit either.

He started strumming another sea song. The others started singing. And I was thankful to just lean back and listen.

It was about dusk when the yellow power boat roared into the anchorage. Harry called out, "Hi!" and began to drop his anchor. Andy nudged me.

Skipper got to his feet. "We'd better stow things now and show Lark those birds she's been waiting to see."

Those birds! I could have done without that exploration. But I couldn't back out.

11

M R. FERGUS RUMBLED OFF IN THE MINI-TRACTOR, leaving the rest of us to see the birds. And it was really dark and spooky in those woods by the time Exploration Birds got under way. Andy couldn't know how glad I was when he caught my hand. Or maybe he could, from the way I clutched his.

"They're not going to hit you this time," he told me. And I was thankful he'd found a nice sensible reason for my nervousness. "When you're on the walk, they seem to come in from each side and not cross over."

WHRRR!

WHRRR!

Several birds WHURTLED in through the trees. And I really hung on, especially when I was ducking.

WHRRR!

"There!" Skipper said, suddenly pinning a startled bird to the forest floor with his flashlight. "That's a rhinoceros auklet."

It seemed about as big as a small duck and nearly as black as . . . *as that Thing I had seen.* There was a light-colored horn rising from high on its beak. Of course! Its rhinoceros horn! And it had a mass of tiny fish dripping from its mouth, making it seem almost silver-whiskered.

"Sandlance . . . needlefish," Andy told us.

"But how . . . ?" Joe started to ask.

"How do they catch that last fish without losing the others? Easy," Andy said. "The *papillae* back on their tongue and palate are saw-edged, with the serrations pointing backward. They impale the fish as they catch them. Neat, eh?"

Only its very last fish had been dropped, I noticed. It was shining there in the light of Skipper's torch.

"Wow!" Joe said. "They're really something."

"I expected them to be bigger," I admitted. "And maybe fiercer looking, after all that noise."

"Oh, the noise is just from their stiff wings beating through the air—the kind of wings they need for underwater flying," Andy explained.

"No big, soft, silent wings like an owl. So they have to land hot, like an interceptor plane. They're not big. But if you think they're not fierce, try touching *him!*"

"No, thank you. I'll take your word for it."

"Well, Lark," Skipper said, "now that you've seen the birds, do you think they were the Gilginamgan's enemy Birds?"

"Of course," I said, pretending I was joking. I didn't know what I thought.

"Then, if that's settled, I think we'd better be getting back to the *Merlin*. We have to be up and at it early tomorrow."

"Lark, would you like to stay with us while Skipper and Joe go off on their cruise?" Mrs. Fergus suggested. "We'd love to have you." I had noticed her casting odd, anxious glances at me during the evening.

"Oh no, thank you," I said. "I'd better learn how to sail while I have the chance." I wanted to get away from Lucy and her menacing brood of islets. I wanted to think things over where I wasn't always glancing out of the corner of my eye, seeing shadows that might not be shadows. And anyway, Mom hadn't belted me off the driftlog just to have me crawl under some other mother's wing.

WHRRR!

"They come in in waves all night," Andy told us.

"Well, we won't wait for the waves," Skipper

said. "All aboard! We'll be back Tuesday, Jenny."

"I'll expect you for dinner. Good sailing!"

Andy walked back through the spooky woods with us, and after making sure I had the Lucy story, he helped us launch the dinghy. Then, when we had climbed back up into the *Merlin*, he blinked some kind of message at us with his flashlight and went off.

"That boy!" Skipper chuckled. "Knows Morse Code, too. Very self-reliant youngster!"

I wished I were. It was terrible to be an uncertain sort of person who didn't quite know what was real and what wasn't real. Why had Mom just belted me off into this terrifying world? It was all Mr. Dennis's idea, I knew. And I hated Mr. Dennis.

The yellow boat was anchored quite near us. But except for a riding light, it was dark. And silent.

Soon the *Merlin* was, too. Yet I could not get to sleep, and not just because the birds kept coming in like rockets. I must have dozed off, though, because it seemed like the middle of the night when, suddenly, I was wide awake.

Perhaps a bird had wakened me. But as I lay there, listening hard, I heard a little splash. And this time I knew it was not a salmon jumping. It was that black canoe again. I was going to sneak a look at it, now that I knew it was a real Fiberglas canoe paddled by a real man.

I did swallow a few times, though, and listen hopefully for some sound from the foc's'le before

I slipped out of the bunk. Then I pulled the sleeping bag around my shoulders and peered out toward the narrow entrance.

There was nothing there. Though the moon was behind a cloud, I could see clearly enough. And there was nothing there.

But I had heard that splash.

WHRRR! A black shape went over like a rocket, straight for Lucy. Then there was silence. But I just knew there was someone out there.

"Well, get out there on deck so you can see the other way!" I ordered myself. And after I'd swallowed a few more times, I did crawl up into the cockpit, keeping very low so the old Indian wouldn't see me.

I looked toward the opening that had been a black ridge and sandbar at low water. And there was nothing there, either.

Then, suddenly, I stifled a scream. There *was* something there, over on the edge of the islet. Something black moved against the darkness of the forest.

The Great Rhinoceros Auklet! I gagged my mouth with the sleeping bag.

Then I sagged in relief as I saw it was just a man, a man in a black wet suit. Harry? I couldn't see his face. But who else could it be? A wide figure in a black wet suit.

Keeping in the shadows as I peered over the gunwale, I could see he had a small bag hanging from his waist—hanging as if it were heavy—and he seemed to have something in his hand, too. Tools? For prying a chest open? Or was he coming off the islet with things he'd stolen from the old chest the Indians had hidden?

"Keep your eyes open!" Winnie had warned me. Through her strange powers, she had known that her great-grandfather's chest was stashed around Lucy and that someone was after it. And she had known that it was my eyes that were going to make the discovery.

WHRRR!

I ducked. But it was the man the bird hit, knocking him over. Stunned by the impact, the bird also fell with a thump. Then, recovering, it fluttered off just as the man made a swipe at it.

It must not have hit him with its head, I thought, because Andy had told me that birds' heads were fragile.

It occurred to me that I had heard more than the thumps. I had heard a rocky clatter. And as I watched from the shadows, almost holding my breath, the man began to search the spot with his shaded light. He picked up bits of something—something he almost hurled into the sea. But he stayed his hand, switched off his light, and vanished into the darkness of the islet.

He had been the presence, I thought, scaring intruders away from the chest—the chest he hadn't wanted the yappy little terrier to sniff out.

On second thought, how could he have been on that islet about eight-thirty when I had been there and still roar into the anchorage in his boat about nine-thirty? It couldn't have been Harry.

No. The presence *had* been the Great Rhinoceros Auklet Spirit. What else could account for this bird hitting Harry? There were no birds breeding on that islet, were there? So why had a bird been flying there? Unless it had been sent there, the way the two big sea gulls had been sent to chase the other sea gulls off the Fergus's roof.

"Spirit power!" I whispered, remembering something.

"*I think maybe he's into spirit power,*" Andy had said of the old Indian. "*If the old man is hiding anything, I think it's a dancing blanket and a dance mask or something. Maybe he shakes rattles and does dances and things.*"

The old Indian, of course! If I hadn't been too terrified to think straight, I'd have realized that the presence was the old Indian in a black dancing blanket and a black bird mask. Of course! In spite of what Andy thought, though, the old man had more than a dancing blanket and the dance mask stashed away on the islet. He had the chest from the old *Mary Brown*. And Harry, researching old shipwrecks for his writing, had got wind of it. Someone had mentioned it to him.

"Bert!"

I just knew that Bert was the one who had told him. He was a relative of Winnie's. So he knew about the old chest. And we'd seen him delivering groceries to the yellow boat. So he knew Harry. And we'd heard Winnie call out, "*Keep away from him!*" just before we'd seen Bert leap her fence. And then Winnie had warned me to keep my eyes open. It all fitted together.

My heart was really thumping as I crawled back into my bunk. Spirit power might be going on here at the Lucy Islands. But something real was going on, too. And I couldn't wait for morning to talk to Andy about it.

It took forever to be morning. Then I had to figure out how I could get ashore before we sailed.

It looked like a sailor's dream in the anchorage, with the sun shining and the pennant whipping out in a fresh breeze. But, fortunately for my purposes, Skipper kept scanning the sky as if he had some doubts. "When you've got a couple of landlubbers crewing for you . . ." he joked as he tried to get more weather reports on the radio.

"It's squally. Fresh sou'westerly, gusting up to fifteen knots," he told us when he'd finally switched off the marine forecasts.

"Fifteen knots!" I said, as if fifteen knots were a wild gale.

"We could lay over for another day," he suggested, about the way he might have suggested eating barnacles for breakfast.

"Oh no!" Joe looked desolated.

"Actually, no," Skipper agreed. "The only way to learn how to handle a little squall is to get out there and do it. And fifteen knots are nothing to the *Merlin*. I could sail her single-handed in fifteen knots . . . You don't get seasick, do you?" he asked me. "You seem a little pale this morning. And I could put you ashore when I pick up my spare can of gas."

"Then you are going ashore?" I said, not committing myself to going or staying until I'd talked to Andy.

Apparently Skipper kept a spare can of gas here; though, from the way he avoided motoring, I didn't see how he was ever going to use up the big red can of gas that already fed the outboard. But I certainly didn't say so. I wanted to get ashore. And I did wonder why Andy wasn't out there on the beach already, waiting to wave us off.

He turned up just in time to help Skipper and me pull up the dinghy. Joe had stayed on board, doing something about getting the sails ready.

"Have I got news for you!" We both burst out with the same whisper as soon as Skipper had headed for the ramp.

"You first," I offered, so he'd have his news off his mind and be able to concentrate on the BIG NEWS.

He turned a wary eye on the yellow boat before taking my hand to pull me toward the barbecue place, well out of earshot.

"There's been a big theft of argillite in town," he said in a very low voice. "I heard guys talking on the CB." A family had returned home from a little holiday only to find several of their best sculptures missing. They had alerted the RCMP. And the Mounties had been searching a few boats.

"Then!" Andy went on. "Rolf got hold of me. Said he couldn't come to take me 'fishing' today. He had a native fishermen's meeting in town. So he'd see me tomorrow." He frowned a bit anxiously over that news, I noticed. Then he pulled a very raggedy white rag out of his pocket and began flicking it at things until we were near the gnarled roots, where it just 'happened' to get caught. And Andy left it.

"The message to the old man," I guessed. "Which sort of brings us to my news."

"Well . . ." he agreed. "The rest of my news isn't all that important. One of those early bird fishermen called in to see if I'd like to go over to town with him in the late morning, for his son's birthday barbecue. I often go over to Ben's. I can always get back with the Coast Guard crew on Monday mornings." He frowned a bit over this news, too, I noticed.

"And you're going?" I asked him, a bit surprised.

"I guess so. Nothing's likely to happen around here tonight, with the Mounties hot on the trail . . . So what's your news?"

"Well . . ." I pulled him up the ramp and along the walk a bit to put us really out of earshot. Then I took a deep breath before I plunged in. I told him everything: the presence on the islet . . . the bird hitting the man in the black wet suit . . .

"I wonder what he picked up so carefully," Andy muttered. "Let's go and find out!"

"But Harry'd see us," I objected.

"Sure. He'd see us skipping stones on the water. And what's suspicious about that? I'm pretty good at it, and I'll show you how. *After we've carefully looked around for the right kind of flat stones.*"

"Wow! . . . But we'd better hurry," I pointed out. "Skipper'll be back soon. He's in a hurry to get out into that fifteen knot wind."

I hadn't meant hurry over that black, slippery rock. But Andy made a big, noisy thing of getting over to the islet. So I did my best and rather surprised myself.

I didn't look like Olympic material at skipping stones, though.

"Hey! I wish you'd do that somewhere else," Joe called out to us. "I don't trust Lark's throwing arm."

"Okay!" Andy surprised me by saying. Then I saw him pat his pocket. He'd found something!

He hauled me back over the slippery rock and across to the ramp before he really let me catch my breath. "Look!" he said, opening his hand.

"Wow!" It was a black chip of something. Like a bird's beak. And it was as smooth as if it had been carved out of black satin rock. "Argillite!"

"Evidence!" Andy said, putting it back into his pocket.

My mind was racing back over the middle of the night. "So he was coming off the islet," I decided, "with stuff he'd stolen from the chest."

"Why does there have to be a chest?"

"But . . ." But everything fitted in if there was a chest. "But . . ." Yes! Why did there have to be a chest? I'd fixed my mind one way, I realized, instead of trimming my sails to the shifting wind. There'd been an argillite robbery in town, hadn't there? And Harry could have been stashing the loot on shore in case of a search of his boat by the Mounties.

"What I can't figure out," Andy said, "is how a guy as fat as Harry could ever slip into a house. Of course he could have had accomplices. Or . . . he could still be a cop, gathering evidence." Again he was frowning. And I thought I knew why. He was wondering if his Indian friends could be involved in the theft. "Look. What do you think we ought to do?"

"Do?" I said, suddenly aghast. It was one thing to be all excited, pretending to be Sherlock Holmes. But—*What do you think we ought to do?* I heard the rumble of the mini-tractor coming along the plank walk. Mr. Fergus was bringing Skipper's can of gas.

"Yes. What do you think we ought to do?" Andy insisted.

"But—aren't the Mounties already doing something? And don't they always get their man?"

"Maybe not without a little help. And that's not their code, you know," he pointed out. "One of the guys on their patrol boat is a friend of mine, and he talks to me sometimes. Their motto is *Maintain the Right . . . without fear, favor or affection.* And you know what that means, don't you? If they— or the people who saw what happened—chicken out because they're afraid of retaliation . . . or because the suspect's someone who's done them a favor . . . or even a friend, for gosh sakes! . . . then they'll never be able to . . . you know—" He broke off, flushing. "So what do we do?"

"Wow!" I said, stunned at suddenly facing reality. Squeal to the police? Go to court and give evidence against a criminal whose gang was going to make you their next target? Even be all wrong and make a fool of yourself in public?

The mini-tractor was bearing down on us.

Andy was still looking at me. "You're the one who saw something," he pointed out. "Anything I say is just hearsay."

"Ready, Lark?" Skipper called out.

"Ready," I answered. "Andy, we can't decide a thing like this in two minutes. And you said nothing's likely to happen tonight. Or tomorrow, I guess. And I'll be back Tuesday. I wish I could stay now," I lied. "But I made Mom a promise. You see, she thinks I . . . sort of . . . chicken out of games and sailing and things. So she said, 'You get out there on that boat and do things!' "

"Oh sure," Andy agreed. "You can't chicken out of things."

Can't you? I thought, despising myself. "And if you decide to do anything, Andy, count me in!"

"Okay," he said; though he didn't look all that cheered by my promise of staunch support. "I don't want to talk to my parents about it. They're not all that keen on my playing detective."

"Parents!" I wailed.

"And anyway, you have to make up your own mind about some things."

"Right!" I agreed.

"All aboard!" Skipper called out as Mr. Fergus lifted the can of gas out of the mini.

"If I didn't have to go!" I wailed, heading for the dinghy.

12

As skipper rowed me and the spare can of gas out to the *Merlin*, I had an awful urge to jump out of the dinghy and swim back to the beach.

The gas was in a squat red can weighing about fifty pounds. And after he and Joe had hoisted it aboard, Skipper said, "I think we'd better leave it down here on deck." He placed it near the cabin hatchway. "It could be a menace on the stern seat if a squall hit; though it doesn't look like gusting up to more than fifteen."

"That's a lot of wind, isn't it?" I said, wondering

if maybe I should make that my excuse for staying ashore after all.

"Oh, the *Merlin's* often out there in fifteen knots, my girl. And it's great sailing!"

The sails were ready. But he still put off hauling up the anchor. "We'll head for Stephens Island," he told us, pointing it out on the chart. "There's good shelter at Squaderee, and a fish-buying camp."

On the chart it looked like Qlawdzeet Anchorage; but he said Squaderee.

"Too bad we can't take time to circumnavigate the island," he went on. "See. You can run down here through Edye Pass and over to Porcher, where there are great beaches."

"And on up past Gull Rocks awash at H.W.," I added, as if I were gung-ho for the sea. All this delay was giving me too much time to change my mind about escaping.

Maybe I could call Andy later, I thought. Skipper had a CB on board, though it did not do any squawking. Like the motor, it was strictly for emergencies. Though with him at the helm, it looked as if the likeliest emergency would come from me tripping over that spare can of gas. Placed nearly amidships, he said it was unlikely to shift. It was "a menace to nobody." Nobody but a girl with big feet.

"Now, Joe," Skipper said, rolling up the chart,

"stand by your anchor, and I'll get the motor going."

Just then we heard the motor start on the yellow boat. Harry waved at us with a hearty, "Hi!" and moved to pull up his anchor.

"As soon as he's out of the way, we'll leave," Skipper told us.

"See you!" Harry called out to us as he gunned his boat toward the entrance.

"Not if we see you first," Skipper muttered as the wash rocked us. Then he started his motor.

"Good sailing!" Andy called, waving from the beach. "See you Tuesday!"

"See you Tuesday!" I felt guiltier than ever as I watched him sprint for the ramp.

We actually did motor out of the anchorage, though maybe that was just to check on the motor. After all, the emergency equipment had to be in good shape.

There was a good breeze from the south as we left the Lucy Islands. And we made southwest for Stephens, close hauled on both the long, gaining tacks and on the shorter losing tacks, with everybody moving up to windward every time we put about.

"It's pretty fresh!" I said, when we'd gone quite a distance. We were really heeling over.

"A fresh breeze is what you want," Skipper said, happy as a sea gull riding the air currents.

It wasn't what I wanted; and I had a sinking feeling that it was going to get much worse. I kept remembering how deep and cold and dark it was down there under the sparkling surface of the sea.

"Well, if you think you can handle the *Merlin*," I said, "I've got that Lucy story to read." Maybe while I was finding out if there *was* a ghost on Lucy Island, I could forget how much we were heeling over. And anyway, the lifejackets were handier in the cabin.

"We'll call you if we need your advice," Skipper joked.

I dropped down into the cabin and dug out the big manila envelope. But before I opened it, I swallowed. Did I really want to read it? The moment I'd touched it, a tingle ran down my spine, and I just hoped it wasn't going to spread into my stomach. But I took a deep breath and pulled out a sheaf of typewritten pages.

Lucy of Lucy Island
Lucy's father was one of the most romantic young sea captains ever to sail up along the Northwest Coast of America. Her mother was a Kaigani chieftainess. So in the eyes of the white people, Lucy grew up as a Colonial young lady. But in native eyes, she was an Indian princess.

"Indian princess!" I gasped. So she *was* the girl in the fringed shift and the totem-decorated canoe-hat. She *was* the girl Winnie had seen.

I shoved the typewritten pages back into the big manila envelope. That was all I wanted to know. It was more than I wanted to know.

There *was* a ghost on Lucy Island; and I'd better face it. I'd vowed to face reality, hadn't I? Even if reality was not quite what Mom had bargained for.

Slanting against the boat's slant, I staggered back out on deck.

"You're not feeling squeamish?" Skipper asked, sizing me up as sharply as if I'd been a sail luffing up.

"Oh no!" I said. "It's just . . . kind of dark down there for reading. And it's too flappy out here."

"So you didn't find out who Lucy was named after?"

"No," I lied. "And anyway, maybe it's time I got out the sandwiches."

"High time!" Joe agreed. "If you don't want to walk the plank."

Still not really thinking of what I was doing, I tripped on the spare can of gas and nearly made my way back into the cabin head first. But I did manage to get the lunch out without pulling the two-burner stove off its stand when I grabbed at it once to save myself from falling.

Lunch was long gone, but I was still swallowing a lot when the wind began to freshen noticeably. And Skipper, who'd been glancing aloft and about, said, "I think we're in for a blow they didn't forecast. We may reef down." As if it was no big deal, really.

But when the first squall hit us, it laid us sharply over.

"Hey!" I said, straining back to offset the sudden heeling.

As soon as the squall had passed, Skipper said, "It's going to blow. And we'll be moving about on deck when it does. So we'll get into our lifejackets and be ready."

"Lifejackets!" I tripped over the gas can again, getting to the cabin for the lifejackets. Long before I had mine properly tied on, Skipper was lifejacketed and starting to reef down.

"Take the tiller, Joe! Bring her up into the wind and KEEP HER THERE! Don't let her go over onto the other tack!"

"Right!" Joe was ready to die hanging onto that tiller.

Skipper kept cautioning him about this and that as he himself lowered the peak of the mains'l until the now-threshing foot of the sail was folded back and forth enough along the boom for him to tie the reef points around it. Then he hauled the peak up again.

"Now there's only about half the mains'l area," he pointed out. "And we'll reduce the others to the storm jib."

"Storm jib!" I croaked. What were we getting

into? "Are we going to head back to Lucy?" I suggested. For all of a sudden, the realities back there seemed a lot less terrifying than the realities of a storm at sea in a twenty-one foot sloop.

"No. We're not far from Squaderee now. And there's good shelter there in the lee of the island." He smiled over at Joe. "You'll make a sailor yet, my lad!"

He didn't have to tell me I wouldn't. "Reef points" and "storm jib" might be exciting words to my brother. They just terrified me. Maybe I had chickened out of facing reality back there at Lucy. But now I had to face it. We were going to sink.

"Lark, up for'd there, you'll see a small canvas bag marked STORM JIB. Take the sail out and pass it up to me through the for'd hatch. When you've done that, go aft and let the jib sheets go. When I give you the word."

"Right." I was glad to have something to do. And with my staggering help, Skipper got the threshing sail down and replaced it with the smaller storm jib.

Though Joe was obviously doing a great job, I was glad when Skipper took the helm again. It had turned really squally, with black patches on the sea ahead. Spray was coming aboard. We were getting wet.

Shifting his gaze from the sea to the rigging, Skipper seemed to be making up his mind about something.

"Look," he said. "We're closer to Stephens now. But with this wind, it could be a bit tricky getting into the anchorage. If we turned back, it'd be better sailing. We'd be running before the wind, on an even keel. And we'd get back in jig time."

"We wouldn't be heeled over?" I said. "Let's turn back, Skipper!" Before we capsized. And sank.

"Yes, I think we will turn back," Skipper said. "Now this is what we're going to do. I'm going to put her over on to the other tack and gradually bring her round before the wind. Stand by!"

Joe moved quickly to man the jib sheets.

"Ready about . . . LEE-o!" Skipper put his helm down to leeward.

I scrambled up to windward to put my weight where it was needed. And as the *Merlin* gathered weigh on the port tack, Skipper began to circle her round, easing off on his main sheet while Joe eased off on his jib sheet.

Concentrated on the maneuver, Skipper hadn't been watching astern. *I* was the one who was free to keep a lookout. But I was too terrified to think of the wind shifting. *I didn't do my job.*

The squall hit us. Coming up from further around to the south, it got behind the mains'l and bashed the boom over in a terrific jibe.

This put us over to port. The main sheet ran out. The end of the boom buried in the breaking crest of a following sea. The sail, now forming a pocket at the clew, began to fill with water, pulling the *Merlin* slowly over onto her beam ends. And the pressure of the sail on the tackle prevented the sail from coming down the mast. The sloop couldn't be brought round before the wind—to take the pressure off—because she wouldn't answer her helm.

Joe hadn't been able to get the jib sheet in, and that sail was threshing wildly.

I was terrified. We were going to capsize. And sink.

Skipper knew we were in trouble. Though the squall wouldn't last, it might last long enough to set us over on our beam ends. We could always take to the dinghy, of course. But now the dinghy had become a menace, too. Coming up on the crest of the following seas, it began to overrun the *Merlin* and bash into her stern. Abandoning ship wouldn't be all that easy. "Keep an eye on the dinghy, Lark! And try to fend her off!"

"Right," I said. But somehow, I didn't jump to do it as Joe would have.

"I'm going to get that jib off. Take the helm, Joe. And hang on to it! Keep it amidships!"

"Right!" Joe sat right down on the deck. And with the helm under his arm, he grasped it with both hands.

The dinghy bashed us again. My job!

I knew you fended things off with the boathook. So I staggered toward the cabin to get it. But I tripped over the combing, grabbed to save myself, bashed the cabin hatch cover forward, and fell in. Picking myself up, I grabbed the butt end of the boathook and pulled it out of its housing. Then, staggering about with that eight foot pole, trying to keep my balance in a heaving, slanting cabin, I lurched backward. The boathook caught on the wires connecting the CB set to the battery; and my lurch pulled the set off its shelf on the bulkhead. The CB landed with a crash on the cabin floor.

Now I really panicked. We wouldn't be able to call for help when we started sinking. But I had to fend off the dinghy. I *had* to fend off the dinghy. So I staggered aft to do it.

The sail was still filling, still pulling us slowly over. Skipper was lying on his back to stay on deck up for'd while he got the threshing sail down.

Suddenly, the slant was so acute that the spare gas can did a somersault. There was a terrific THUD behind me. And I screamed.

Skipper knew it was that heavy gas can that had shifted. He thought it might have hit one of Joe's legs. So he abandoned his threshing sail and began to scramble aft to see what had happened.

But what he didn't know was that I had bashed the hatch cover open while I was falling into the cabin to get the boathook. And looking straight aft to check on Joe, he stepped into the open hatch. His hand missed the hatch combing, and he pitched down onto the cabin floor, striking his shoulder

hard against the bunk.

I heard a groan and a "Bloody Hell!"

Now we *were* going to sink!

But just then the squall passed. And the *Merlin* slowly began to right herself on her new course. The sea spilled out of the sail. And I began to breathe again.

But Skipper was really hurt. And—thanks to my clumsiness—the CB was out of action. We couldn't call for help. Faint with pain, he made his way up into the cockpit.

"It's a dead run now for Lucy," he said. He scanned the sea and the sky. "The squalls seem to have passed. I think it's settled down to a good, strong, steady sou'wester. I'll take the helm, Joe, while you put the jib back on."

"Can't we use the motor?" I pleaded.

Skipper caught his breath. "That fall must have shaken me. I'd forgotten all about the bloody motor. In this breeze, we could get there just as fast under sail. But under the circumstances, it'll be good business to use the motor. We'll start the motor and bring her up into the wind and get the sail off."

Another maneuver? Another squall hitting us right in the middle of it? I almost held my breath while Joe started the outboard. But it went. Skipper brought her round into the wind. And we got the sail off.

Joe took the helm as we headed for Lucy Island—with a skipper who might faint at any minute, I knew. He looked awful to me, stretched out on one of the seats in the cockpit with a sleeping bag over him. And there was no way we could call for help.

I just did not trust the weather. Nor the motor. I kept catching my breath as I listened to it.

I can't have held my breath most of the way back to Lucy. But it certainly felt as if I did. Though the island was in plain sight all the time, it never seemed to get any closer. And you didn't exactly whoosh through a breaking, following sea with a six horsepower motor pushing four tons of sailboat. You planed ahead on a crest. But then you almost seemed to stop as you slid back into the trough. I watched the sun sinking, with clouds building up, and knew daylight wasn't going to last forever.

Skipper might not last either, I thought, panicking every time I looked at him stretched out there. "He looks bad," I mouthed to Joe.

"Yeh," he whispered back. "Maybe we should call the Coast Guard on the CB. They've got a helicopter."

"It's smashed," I told him.

"The helicopter?"

"No. The CB."

"Smashed?" Joe glared at me as if it was my fault. Which it was.

"SH!" I hissed at him. No use upsetting Skipper.

"We've got flares," Joe mumbled. "But who'd see them?"

The world did seem to be empty, except for the *Merlin*. The Sunday fishermen had all gone home after the blow. There were lonely little lights flashing away off to port and starboard. And ahead of us, Lucy's light was raking the clouds. But there was no watch up there in the tower, I knew; and from where we were, the keepers' houses were behind a wooded knoll. It seemed awfully lonely out there on that darkening sea.

Skipper mumbled something, over the noise of the engine.

"Yes?" I said, hanging over him; maybe I thought I was going to hear the last words of a dying man. But it was Joe he wanted to talk to, about getting into the anchorage. So I had to take the tiller, even though I just knew that outboard was going to konk out while I had it. Or a submerged peak was going to rise up, dead ahead.

But when Joe took the tiller back, it seemed even worse, because then I could think about even worse things.

It all came back to ME. If I hadn't chickened out of facing reality, I'd be back there with Andy, deciding what to do. And without me there, on the *Merlin*, failing to keep a lookout during the maneuver . . . and bashing the hatch cover open . . .

and smashing the CB, Skipper and Joe would be enjoying a sail back to Lucy. Instead of putt-putting along with Skipper hurt.

Oh! What was the use of thinking?

But how could you stop thinking?

13

NEVER HAD THAT BIG, SOLID LIGHTHOUSE LOOKED better to anyone than it looked to me when we finally started putt-putting along the north shore of Lucy, heading for the anchorage.

But why hadn't the Ferguses seen us from the house? Though if they had, I realized, they'd just think Skipper had turned back because of the weather. "If only we could use the flashlight to tell them what's happened!" I muttered. But who knew Morse Code? Except Andy. And he was probably off at his friend's barbecue. Why hadn't Joe spent his time learning Morse Code instead of knots?

There was a power boat roaring toward us from the Passage. But it was probably just Harry, who'd make Skipper feel worse.

Joe kept close in because of the rocky islets off to starboard. "You'll have to ready the anchor," he told me. "Release it. Make sure it's fixed to its cable. See it doesn't foul anything. And for Pete's sake, don't go overboard with it!"

"I won't," I said, clambering for'd to do it. "Remember that rock!" I warned my brother.

"You just do your job!" he warned me, cutting his motor.

Somehow, I did. The anchor splashed in. The chain rattled over the side. The rope ran out. And Joe leaped for'd to see that it was holding.

"We've made it, Skipper!" he called out.

But Skipper had fainted, I guess. Anyway, he didn't answer.

"Look," I said. "I'll go for help. And I'm not waiting while you check on your anchor and get things shipshape and navy fashion. I'm not waiting for the dinghy."

I dived in. It was panic, I think, and not sudden courage. I just wanted to get to somebody who could look after Skipper.

But wow! The water was so cold it took my breath away. And all I could think of was how deep and dark and cold it was under me. But somehow I made it to the beach. And if I heard a motor roaring round to the cove, it didn't register. I just staggered out of the Polar Seas and headed for the ramp.

I caught my breath again as I went into the woods. It seemed awfully black in there, with all those spruce trees thrusting up into the darkening sky.

I hadn't even thought of a flashlight. But I could see the plank walk as I scurried along it, looking straight ahead. I didn't dare to look sideways, now that I knew there *was* a ghost on Lucy Island. But I could sense the trees reaching out for me. And I couldn't seem to go fast.

I was rushing up a slope when my foot hit a torn part of the wire netting and I went sprawling.

I must have screamed.

"Hi!" The shout came from somewhere away behind me, muffled by the trees and the deep green mosses. My first thought was "Harry!"

Harry would pounce on me and strangle me and throw my body under the plank walk. Yet I couldn't seem to move to escape him.

"Hey! Lark!"

"Andy!" It was Andy, coming up behind like the Good Forester or something. I was so relieved that even my face dropped down onto the plank walk. I just lay there until he came up.

"I'm going for Mom," he said, giving me a yank up before he raced on, leaving me to get out of the woods all alone. Without the rush of purpose, the place seemed infinitely scarier. There wasn't just one ghost on Lucy Island. There were a dozen; and I caught every last one of them out of the corner of my eye.

Then I was out in the open again.

"Take a hot bath!" Mrs. Fergus ordered as she passed me near the house steps. And I was thankful it was an order. I didn't have to think of what to do next. Someone else had taken over. I heard the mini-tractor starting up. Then Andy passing me, stopped long enough to say, "I'm going back with Mom. She's a nurse, so she can talk to the doctor on the CB."

"But it's smashed!" I wailed.

"The one on the boat I came in," he said, and raced off. I was alone again.

I took the hot bath, found jeans and a shirt. And I was making some hot chocolate when Andy came back.

"Skipper's okay," he said. "Just a wrenched shoulder. They're taking him into the hospital. And Mom's going with him."

"Thank Heaven!" I said. He couldn't know how relieved I was, because he didn't know how much it was all my fault. "You said 'the boat I came in'. So you did go to town."

"Yes," he said, frowning. Then he plunged into an account of it. "I borrowed Ben's bike, the way I always do—before the barbecue. And I tracked down Rolf at the fishermen's meeting."

"And . . . ?"

"Well, he looked a bit worried. Said he'd try to get out tonight, after all, to check on the old man."

"Then . . ."

"Then. Wow! I didn't know what to do. So I rode back to Ben's by way of the Coast Guard Station where the police patrol boat is. My friend saw me hanging around and came out. And I . . . sort of said I'd heard there'd been a big argillite theft. And he said they'd caught the thief."

"Harry!" I just knew it was Harry.

"No. A juvenile. That's all he said. 'A juvenile.' "

"But—" I'd been so sure it was Harry.

"Kevin—the Mountie—asked me what I was doing in town and how I was going to get back. Said if I didn't want to stay over, I could go back with him. He was going over to be ready for some early morning fishing on his day off. So I came back with him. And he's taking Skipper."

"Wow!" I said. "So our whole case has bombed out."

"Looks like it. And am I glad I didn't mention it to my parents! But!"

"But what?" I asked him.

"I still think there's something going on around here. We're not finished yet."

"We're not?" What did he have in mind now?

"No, we're not. We're going to sneak over onto that islet tonight and see what's going on."

"Okay," I agreed. Get out there and do things, my mother had said. Though I wasn't sure this was just what she had meant.

"Soon as things have settled down in the anchorage, we'll get over there. Dad'll think we're staying on the *Merlin* with Joe. And Joe'll think we're at the house. Nobody will know we're over there."

"Good," I said, trying not to sound shaky about nobody's knowing we were over on that islet where even the birds didn't go.

It was getting really dark by the time Andy decided we should set out. Peering through the bushes, we'd seen Joe hoist the riding light up onto the mast. And now the light in the *Merlin's* cabin told us that he was turning in—though he probably had the alarm clock set to wake him up every so often for a log watch. It seemed lonely in the anchorage. Only the startling whurtle of the birds coming in from sea shattered the quiet gloom of Lucy Island.

With the tide rising, we had to roll up our jeans and go over barefoot. I tried not to think of how we were going to be cut off soon by the water.

We pushed our way through the dense undergrowth into the clearing. And now it was really spooky. Spooky and utterly, utterly quiet. As soon as our eyes were accustomed to the gloom, Andy whispered, "If you were stashing loot around here, where would you put it?" Then, without waiting for an answer, he crept silently toward the HOLE.

I followed close behind him. But I just could

not put my hands down into that fibrous black stuff.

"We'll have to use the flashlight," he told me. "But I've got a dark cloth fixed over it. And we can keep the light down in the hole."

"Maybe . . . I could hold the flashlight," I offered.

"Well . . . here. But keep it low! And hold it steady, for gosh sakes!"

WHRRR!

I dropped the flashlight.

"It's only the birds coming in," Andy snapped, groping down deeper to retrieve the flashlight. "Hey!" he said in an excited whisper. "I've found something!"

It was a small canvas bag with something heavy in it. Like the bag the man in the wet suit had had tied on.

Andy loosened the drawstrings and we saw an argillite totem pole.

"Wow!" I whispered.

"Sorry it's not the chest from the old *Mary Brown*," he whispered back, sounding very excited. "My guess is that someone's been stealing argillite in Prince Rupert and caching it here until things are clear for a getaway. And Harry's involved, either as part of the racket or as an undercover cop. Either way, it would explain why he didn't want a little terrier snooping around on shore; they're terrible for digging around the burrows. My guess is that there's more of the stuff down there. And I have this feeling that tonight is the night for the pickup. They've caught the juvenile who was lifting the stuff. And he might talk." He carefully put the canvas bag back in the hole and switched off the light.

"But what's the use of finding it if you're just going to leave it down there?" I protested.

"To watch. And see what happens. A cache is just circumstantial evidence if nobody's near it." He began looking about for a good place to hide.

"A stakeout!" I whispered.

"Yeh. Where nobody'll spot us." He finally settled on a terribly gloomy spot behind heavy underbrush. "I hope you're not a sneezer."

"Well . . . if it gets too cold . . ." I suggested. Though I was wearing a warm jacket of his mother's.

"That's why I brought the rugs." He undid the packsack on his back and handed me one.

WHRRR! WHRRR! WHRRR! The rocket-winged fishermen were really hitting Lucy. And it was getting awfully dark on our islet. I was thankful when Andy took my hand. "Now just shut up!" he whispered. "You never know who's hovering around."

That was what worried me.

After a long, long time, we heard a power boat

come into the anchorage. Harry?

Andy squeezed my hand. And I knew it meant, "Shut up!"

It seemed a century, but it couldn't have been more than twenty minutes before Andy squeezed my hand again, hard. And, peering through the underbrush, I made out a figure coming into the clearing.

Rolf! I just knew how Andy must be feeling. But Rolf didn't go near the hole. He went silently on through the opening that led to the next clearing and the forest beyond that. I could sense Andy sagging in relief.

"He said he'd try to get out to check on the old man tonight," Andy whispered. "Guess he couldn't get here any sooner. Gosh! I hope he's hidden the dinghy he came ashore in!"

Then nothing happened. For hours and hours, it seemed, nothing happened—except pins and needles in my left foot. And I was afraid to shift for fear I'd make a noise.

Finally we heard another power boat come into the anchorage. Now it *would* be Harry.

I almost held my breath as we waited and waited. But nothing happened. Maybe it was just Andy's friend back from taking Skipper, I thought ... Or maybe it *was* Harry, after all. He had certainly waited until the middle of the night to come ashore the night before, when he could be sure that people in the other boats were all asleep. *Had* he been caching that loot on the islet when I'd seen him? And would he pick it up tonight?

I realized I hadn't heard a bird for ages. So it must be very, very late. It was quiet. Unnaturally quiet! And the clouds kept moving across the moon, changing the shadows. I began to feel a presence. A terrible, silent presence. And the clearing seemed to be picking up a weird motion. A tree seemed to move. A shadow began creeping along the ground.

I'm looking too hard, I told myself. So I closed my eyes to rest them for a minute.

I must have fallen asleep. And dreamed I heard another boat coming into the anchorage. At least, I thought it was just a dream. Then a rattlesnake was shaking its tail at me.

I opened my eyes. Stifled a scream. Someone was slipping toward the HOLE. And I heard Andy catch his breath.

Rolf!

Andy squeezed my hand in a hard, "Shut up!" And I kept silent as a stump while the young Indian groped around in the fibrous black stuff until he pulled out the small, heavy canvas bag. He groped about a bit more, and pulled out another. So the cache of argillite was his! I squeezed Andy's hand in sympathy. I knew how he must be feeling.

"Maybe it's their stuff from the old *Mary Brown* chest," I whispered, to cheer him up.

Then I realized that the rattlesnake was still

shaking its tail at me. I glanced toward the sound. And this time I did scream. For, with a leap, a giant black bird appeared. Then, with a low burrow moan, it moved off in slow, ponderous hops, with the rattle coming louder and louder from one of its wings.

"*The Great Rhinoceros Auklet!*" I guess I shrieked it, right after my scream.

Rolf slipped back into the shadows. And another figure rushed into the clearing—a man in a black wet suit.

"Harry!" I burst out.

14

B UT IT WASN'T HARRY. THIS MAN WAS TALL AND
slim.

"Kevin!" Andy said, leaping up since
I'd already blown our cover. And he sounded almost accusing. "So you weren't coming out here
just fishing for *fish!*" The story about fishing on
his day off had been just a cover. Maybe the juvenile thief they'd caught had tipped him off. Or
maybe the Mountie had just suspected that something was going on round Lucy Island. Without
Andy telling him. And like a flash I saw what was
bugging Andy. It looked as if he had sneakily set

up this capture of his Indian friend. I felt terrible for him.

Rolf emerged from the shadows; while the huge bird just kept circling the eerie clearing in his ponderous hops, moaning the way Andy had told me the birds moaned.

Andy must have noticed that my teeth were chattering. He switched on his dimmed flashlight and turned it on the bird. "It's just Rolf's grandfather, for gosh sakes!" he snapped at me. And I could see that it was a man, a man in a black bird costume and a black bird mask. Then he turned the light on the canvas bags that lay near the hole.

"I'm RCMP Corporal Blaine," the Mountie said formally to Rolf. "I want to see what's in those bags." He spoke very quietly.

Rolf picked one up and handed it over. Corporal Blaine looked inside it and put it down again. Then he put a hand on Rolf's shoulder. "Rolf, we've known each other for a long time. But it's my duty to put you under arrest on suspicion of being in possession of stolen goods. I warn you that you need not make any statement, but anything you do say will be given in evidence against you at your trial."

"But I didn't do nothing," Rolf said, looking very unhappy.

"I'm sure he didn't," Andy said, looking even more unhappy.

And because I felt terrible for him, and maybe

because I have a one-track mind anyway, I burst out, "It was Harry! I saw him last night on the beach with that bag."

"Who are you?" Corporal Blaine asked.

"Lark Doberly. I'm on Skipper's *Merlin*. And I came out on deck last night and saw a bird knock him over, and he dropped a piece of argillite. Andy's got the evidence."

Andy pulled the black slate chip out of his pocket and showed it to the Mountie while I gabbled out the whole thing—even about Harry keeping the yappy little terrier from coming ashore to sniff out the cached loot because terriers were terrible for digging around burrows. Then, suddenly, I stopped gabbling. "But you caught the thief, didn't you?" I said. "A juvenile." Then another thought hit me. "Was it Bert?"

"Why? What do you know about Bert?"

"Well . . . he knew about the chest and—" But there was no chest, was there? It was just me and my one-track mind again. It was clear that this cache had nothing to do with the wreck of the *Mary Brown*. But it still had something to do with Harry, and maybe Bert. And anyway, maybe catching the thief was just something else the Mountie had told Andy, to put people off guard. "I mean . . . nothing. I just saw him leaping fences and delivering groceries to the yellow boat."

The old man stopped dancing. "I know. I see," he said in a low, hoarse voice. "Some nights I see.

Fat white man come many times. I know that man. Man in yellow boat. No good, that one. He put Indian things with bird spirits down in hole. This night I tell Rolf get spirits out of hole."

"Yeh," Rolf agreed. "He thinks . . . you know, Corporal." He moved his hands in helpless acceptance of the ways of Old People.

"He sent for Rolf," Andy said, in stout defense of his friends. "I know. I relayed the message. And he was probably dancing to appease those bird spirits that had been put down in the hole."

A motor started up in the anchorage. The Mountie's head jerked toward the sound. "Come along with me, Rolf," he said, more urgently than he had spoken before.

Rolf started across the clearing without a word; while his grandfather once more began dancing and moaning and shaking his rattle.

Suddenly there was a roar from the anchorage. Someone was gunning his boat toward the entrance.

"Don't touch a thing!" the Mountie called out. And he dashed for the beach, with us right behind him. "Andy, keep an eye peeled! I'll alert your father."

We saw the yellow boat roar out, leaving the *Merlin* and the other boat rocking under their riding lights. Harry must have seen or heard something on the islet, I thought, and panicked. He was getting the heck out of there, under cover of darkness. I saw Joe come out on the deck of the *Merlin*.

WHRRR!

WHRRR!

In the dark of predawn, Lucy Island was exploding with the rocket-winged fishermen.

And Harry was escaping!

The Mountie turned to Rolf. "Wait until I come back or you hear from the RCMP!" he said before he dived in.

"Sure, I'll be here," Rolf called after him. "I didn't do nothing. Why should I run away?"

"Kevin knows the Indians can be trusted," Andy whispered to me. "Rolf won't try to escape. Anyway, he didn't do it. And all the old man was doing was looking after the bird spirits. He'll see that no one makes off with that stuff before the RCMP patrol boat gets here. And so will we!" He looked at me, and his voice picked up excitement. "At least we know now that Harry wasn't an undercover cop. Or he wouldn't have roared off like that. My guess is that he's the possessor of stolen goods. Not Rolf!"

"But he'll get away!" I wailed. "And it's all my fault. I screamed. If I hadn't screamed, he'd have come ashore and been arrested."

The island exploded with another WHRRR! WHRRR! WHRRR! of birds.

"Maybe he was underwater, coming ashore for

the loot when you screamed," Andy said, to cheer me up. "More likely it was my light he saw, when he surfaced. After I switched it on, he'd just about have had time to make it back to the boat and roar off. Wonder if he had a float for that heavy stuff."

"Never mind that!" I snapped at him. "He's going to get away. And it is my fault."

"He won't get very far, once Kevin gets on the blower," Andy said. "Every patrol on the Coast'll know about him, on both sides of the border."

I sagged in relief, until Andy added, "You'll have to go to court, I guess, and give evidence. After all, you're the one who saw him on this islet with that canvas bag last night."

I opened my mouth to protest. But nothing seemed to come out. Then I swallowed, and said, "So I'll have to go to court and give evidence." As if it was no big deal.

"You're really something!" Andy said.

The Mountie had climbed up into his fishing boat. He disappeared inside for a few minutes, then he started his motor, pulled up his anchor, and waved at us. He was off to *Maintain the Right*.

Rolf waved and slipped back into the forest.

"See you, Rolf," Andy called after him. Then he turned back to me. "You're really something!" he said, again.

"But I'm not really, Andy," I admitted, suddenly sagging with tiredness and honesty. "I'm scared stiff half the time. I chicken out of everything. And I'm going to turn into a beanpole as well as a weirdo."

"You mean your height?" Andy asked, tackling one thing at a time. "You don't know much, do you?"

"Maybe not. But I know I'm a beanpole."

"Sure. Because girls go on their gaining tack sooner than boys do. Look!" said Encyclopedia Jr., "at thirteen a girl will have completed ninty-five percent of her growth, while a boy may not go into his growth spurt until he's fourteen."

So he did worry about his height.

"In a couple of years, Joe and I will be calling you 'Shorty.' "

"Oh Andy!" I said, "You're the best thing that ever happened to me."

"Sure," he agreed. "I gave you the chance to finally eat prickled sea urchins. And I got the Lucy story for you, didn't I? Hey, what did you think of Lucy of Lucy Island?

"Well . . . I . . . sort of chickened out of reading it."

"What was there to chicken out of?"

"Well . . . the ghost."

"What ghost? There was no ghost in that story." He was looking at me as if I were the Stupid Monster.

"Hey!" Joe called out from the *Merlin*. "What's going on around here?"

"Come and get us and we'll tell you," Andy called back. "And watch out for the birds!"

"Okay!" Joe called back. "When I've checked on everything around here."

Andy turned back to me. "What ghost?" he insisted.

"Well . . ." The quiet was broken by another explosion of birds. I shivered.

"What ghost?"

So I blurted out the whole thing about Winnie's ghost girl in the fringed shift and the Northwest Coast Indian canoe-hat, in the painting. And before I knew what I was doing, I was telling him about Pearly Plunkl. "So don't you see?" I almost yelled at him. "I'm going to turn into a weirdo, like Winnie."

"Not if you can't paint," he pointed out. "Look, maybe there *are* invisible playmates and ghosts and spirits and things. Don't you even know that some scientists are postulating an invisible world of matter vibrating at such a high frequency that we can't tune in on it? Even though it may be all around us."

"No," I admitted. I didn't even know "postulating." "You mean there may be spirits and ghosts and things?" I challenged him.

"There may be," he admitted, a little reluctantly.

"Then why are you so up-tight telling me not to tell anybody about your father and the Great Sea Gull Spirit?"

"Well . . . I guess because a lot of people might think . . . You know what people might think! But, if they really are there, well . . . maybe they're a source of energy—"

"—to be harnessed like the wind," I broke in. "Maybe if you go along with them—the way your father did—maybe they'll help you and not lay you flat, like when a squall hits you." I knew what I meant, even if I didn't make it all that clear to Andy. It was what *you* did about the Other World; how you didn't just pretend it wasn't there; how you didn't just sit there like a bump on a log, letting things terrify you.

I saw Joe put the ladder overside to come off in the dinghy. No doubt he had everything shipshape and navy fashion on the *Merlin*.

"Maybe you're sensitive or something," Andy went on. "But I sure don't think you're a weirdo."

"You don't? You really don't?"

"No. Just kind of dumb, maybe, going round half-scared all the time and bottling it all up."

"But, Mom wants me to bottle it all up. And put a cork in it. She wants me to face reality."

"So. Did you ever face the reality of really talking to her about these things?"

"Well . . . no . . . I guess not," I admitted, stifling a yawn. "But I will." For the first time in my life, I was going to really talk to my mother. And I'd stop escaping into myself . . . into my crazy imagination . . . into childhood, maybe, with a phantom father . . . into wanting the family to stay just as it was forever. Things did change. And if you had any sense, you trimmed your sails to the shifting wind, and maybe even tried to exult in it, the way Skipper did.

"You know," I told Andy. "Maybe I'll even talk to Mr. Dennis."

"Who's Mr. Dennis?"

"Oh, just a teacher the other kids think is the greatest thing since bubble gum."

"I hope you know what you're talking about. I sure as heck don't."

"You know what?" I said, changing the subject. "I'll bet Bert was delivering stolen argillite to Harry with the groceries." Then, suddenly, I really sagged with tiredness. All I wanted was my bunk and my sleeping bag. After a good sleep, I thought, I'd read *Lucy of Lucy Island*.

Then Joe was maneuvering the dinghy in; Andy was pulling it up; and I was getting aboard like an old hand.

Reality could be pretty exciting, I decided, as we set out for the *Merlin*.

But . . . What was reality? I wondered, and still wonder every time I think of the most wonderful, scary, weird, exciting week in my whole life.

LUCY OF LUCY ISLAND

LUCY'S FATHER WAS ONE OF THE MOST ROMANTIC young sea captains ever to sail up along the Northwest Coast of America. Her mother was a Kaigani chieftainess. So in the eyes of the white people, Lucy grew up as a colonial young lady. But in native eyes, she was an Indian princess.

Capt. Wm. Henry McNeill first came to these waters in 1825 as the twenty-two-year-old skipper of the Boston trading brig *Convoy*. A master mariner at the age of twenty, he had been born in Edinburgh and trained in the Royal Navy. From one of His Majesty's ships off the New England coast, he had watched the battle between the

British *Shannon* and the American *Chesapeake;* and he had noted in his diary that the battle lasted fifteen minutes.

Then, scenting adventure in the New World, he had thrown in his lot with the Boston men trading along the wild Northwest Coast in defiance of the Hudson Bay Company and its Royal Charter.

In the autumn of 1830, as master of the fully manned and armed Yankee brig *Llama,* he cleared again for the North Pacific by way of Tahiti, Samoa, Hawaii, and California.

"We'll show those Company men how to trade," he said; and his eyes sparkled. For along with the usual blankets and kettles, firearms and ammunition, he had taken on toys. He had jumping jacks, little wagons, whistles, and squeaking dogs and cats. "The Indian families will love them!" he gloated.

It was May when he sailed off the west coast of Vancouver Island, bound for Alaska. And he was sure the Company's ships would challenge a Boston trader on that coast. But he had reached Dixon Entrance—the wild straits separating the Queen Charlotte Islands from the Alaskan islands—before he fell in with the Company's *Dryad* and *Vancouver.* And the three merely exchanged a salute of big guns and passed on "on their lawful occasions."

Only, according to the HBC, the *Llama's* occasions were not lawful. A Royal Charter had given the Company exclusive right to the Indian trade along this coast. The Boston man was trespassing.

"Aye, but not for long," the HBC ships' companies agreed. The Yankee brig would be taken care of, with no trouble at all to the Company or its captains.

Unwary of anything but the natural hazards of these notoriously perilous seas, Capt. McNeill readily took on board an Indian chief who hailed him and offered to pilot the ship to a safe anchorage. And when he reached the "safe anchorage," he dropped anchor. But the hawser snapped. And hundreds of canoes put out to plunder the wreck that seemed imminent; for a grounded ship, like a beached whale, belonged to the chief on whose shore it had washed up.

But McNeill had not dared the mighty HBC to be thwarted by an Indian. Promptly tossing the piratical chief overboard, he hoisted sail and made for a friendlier harbor. And there he found not only prime furs for his owners, but also a beautiful Kaigani chieftainess for himself.

The Kaigani, an Alaskan branch of the seagoing Haida—the haughty Lords of the Coast—readily accepted the fine young white sea chief as a suitable husband for their princess. And with proper Haida ceremonial, the captain married the lady and carried her off in the *Llama*. Now, like most of the Hudson Bay Company traders, *he* had staunch relatives among the coastal natives. Even Chilkat pirates would think twice before offending the lordly Haida.

All summer he traded along the coast, more generous with his trades goods than the Company men were. The jumping jacks and the squeaking dogs and cats were an enormous success with the fun-loving, child-loving natives. And the *Llama* prospered.

The Company gentlemen seethed. They complained to the *Llama*'s owners in Boston. They ordered McNeill off their coast, though always with a wary eye on his able crew, his big guns, and the high-ranking lady standing haughtily at the rail with her silver earrings glinting under her decorated canoe-hat.

McNeill laughed at them and went on trading. Not until the wild gales sent the fur-trading Indians into their winter villages for their great ceremonials did he sail for Hawaii with a valuable cargo of pelts.

He cruised the South Seas, still trading. But with spring, he was back in the North Pacific.

Since it was more profitable to treat than to fight, the Company had begun negotiating with the *Llama*'s owners in faraway Boston, to buy the ship.

"And her captain with her," HBC men had agreed with one another.

Unaware of this possibility, McNeill spent

March trading in Puget Sound. And when the British brig *Cadboro* drove him away from Fort Vancouver, he answered with his guns. But he also headed north once more. After all, his wife had relatives to visit. And the relatives had furs to sell.

On his way north, he anchored briefly in Camosun Bay at the southeast tip of Vancouver Island; for the spot had won his heart. "It's a bonnie land," he told his Kaigani lady as his eyes scanned the parklike area that would some day be known as Victoria.

The weather was perfect. The wild flowers were brilliant under the great oak trees.

"If the Company men had half the good sense they think they have, they would build a fort here," he said. "Their precious charter won't hold forever in the Oregon Country." They, too, would be driven away from Fort Vancouver. They, too, would have to head north.

That summer brought the word from Boston. The Company had bought the *Llama* and her cargo. Her captain was offered another Boston ship.

But the HBC had a counter offer. "Come along with your ship, Captain!" they urged him. "You'd do fine with the Company."

McNeill agreed. He liked the ship. He liked the wild coast. So he changed the flag on the *Llama*, settled his family at Nisqually in Puget Sound, and went on trading.

Lucy, the fourth of his children, was such a little girl the first time he took her to Camosun Bay that she jumped when he received a salute of guns from the bastion of the newly established HBC trading post; he was now skipper of the Company's *Beaver*, a sailing brig turned paddlewheel steamer—the first steamer in the North Pacific. Then with her sister Helen, she scampered about the lovely parklike area she was always to love. And her dark eyes sparkled under her canoe-hat; her totem-crested earrings glinted in the sunshine. For, by the native matrilineal laws of heredity, she was a Kaigani princess.

But she was a Scot, too, with the "poetic feeling for wooded and watered landscape which is the birthright of the Scot."

Not long after that visit, Capt. McNeill sailed the *Cowlitz* to England for supplies for Fort Simpson, and the company steamer moved his family north to the Fort itself. It was at this time that Lucy first saw the lovely little island that was to be named for her. For Fort Simpson Indians still paddled over to *Laghspannah*—as they called the island—to their traditional abalone reefs.

It was at this time, walking with them along their old trail, that she first saw sunlight slipping through the spruce trees to turn the green mosses and the green ferns and the wild green lily-of-the-valley into a wonderland of green light. Camped with the Indians at night, she first heard the startling WHURTLE of the sea birds; and before sunup, she heard the island explode with its rocket-winged fishermen.

Capt. McNeill arrived with the supplies from England. And he had his family on board when he brought out the northern furs. They sailed to Fort Vancouver on the Columbia River, where they unloaded the furs and took on wheat and other farm produce for Fort Simpson and Alaska. Then, as HBC agent to the Russian post at Sitka, McNeill settled his family in there for the winter. And Lucy was wide-eyed at the splendors of the Russian Governor's balls.

For the next few years, the McNeills lived inside the palisades at Fort Stikeen; and the natives were unfriendly to the white men. Yet, when the Company decided to abandon the post, the Stikeens were furious. And the family had to walk out through hostile lines of armed and war-painted Indians. But no one offered harm to the white Chief or to his haughty Kaigani lady and her children; for in native eyes, those children belonged to the Kaigani; and the Kaigani were a branch of the fierce Haida, the unchallenged Lords of the Coast.

Capt. McNeill was transferred to the northern tip of Vancouver Island, where the Company had found coal for its ships. There he built Fort Rupert. And though he was in charge of the post, he was often away at sea. It was from Fort Rupert that Lucy, now a teen-ager, finally went to live in the beautiful parklike area at Camosun Bay.

"You're going away to school, lassie," her father told her. "You and your sisters."

"To Mrs. Staines' school?" Lucy gasped, caught between excitement at going and shyness of the Staines, about whom there were so many rumors. Then she began to giggle; for Lucy, like her mother and her mother's relatives, had a great sense of the ridiculous. And the Rev. Mr. Staines was ridiculous.

On his way to Camosun to be Fort Chaplain, he had been presented to an Hawaiian king. And always concerned to impress people with his station in life, he had dressed his one manservant in the splendid livery he had brought along for just such an occasion, while he himself went clothed in the somber dignity of his Church robes.

"Mr. Staines!" the king had exclaimed, moving cordially to shake hands with the splendid manservant.

"Savages!" Mr. Staines had scoffed, though under his breath, of course.

Lucy hadn't heard all the gossip about Mrs. Staines. Oh, she had heard of the black skirts and the rows of corkscrew curls at each side of her face. She had heard of the lady's arrival. "Where are the streets?" Mrs. Staines had demanded when the ship's officers had finally set her down in the mud near the fort gate. Where was the house suitable for people of their station?

What she had not heard was that Mrs. Staines had also demanded to know where were the fort's *ladies*. She had gazed with horror at the native wives. And her horror had deepened when she discovered that they had not even gone through Christian rites. A "heathen" marriage was no marriage at all in her eyes. So the women were sinners as well as savages. And she was expected to turn their daughters into respectable young ladies? The prospect made her shudder.

The schoolroom had made her shudder, too. For the Fort had allotted part of Bachelors' Hall to the Staines and their charges during the day. Bachelors' Hall, where the young gentlemen of the fort took their sometimes boisterous evening relaxation, was clearly a den of iniquity. And her boarders had to sleep overhead!

The McNeill girls went to Victoria in a great totem-crested canoe manned by northern Indians who dared the treacherous Seymour Narrows and the even more treacherous Yuculta raiders chanting their wild sea songs.

Lucy dared the perils of Mrs. Staines's school a little more timidly.

"Lucy McNeill," the schoolmistress greeted her young boarder from Fort Rupert. And her severe glance noted the "savage" ornaments. "Those barbarian baubles will have to go!"

"Oh no!" Lucy cupped her hands protectingly over the beautiful earrings that marked her rank as princess.

"Young ladies do not wear earrings."

"But . . . they do." Her mother ought to know what young ladies wore. *She* was a very great lady with slaves and servants; *she* was most concerned about the proper dress and proper behavior of a girl with chiefs' blood.

Mrs. Staines eyes narrowed. Her lips pursed. Her corkscrew curls trembled on both sides of her face. She would teach these little savages not only to read and write and cipher, but also how to conduct themselves with modesty and dignity.

She was an excellent teacher to the girls, who had already been taught by their fathers. And she did dress her charges as she felt young ladies of the new colony should be dressed. But she could no more repress the high spirits of her girls than she could stop the howling of the fort dogs or the revels of the young gentlemen.

One Saturday night, when the bachelors and their guests had decided to "escort the Queen to Windsor Castle," they "galloped" about the Hall so noisily that the "sleeping" girls above decided to get in on the fun. With careful aim, they poured water from their crude washbasins through the cracks down on the revellers. And when word of the prank reached Mrs. Staines's ears, she used it to point up the shocking conditions of her boarding school. If the Company would not provide her young ladies with something better for their ablutions than discarded pans from the dairy, she said, how could *she* instill dignity?

Schooldays were happy for Lucy. But they didn't last long. Before the year was out, and she was sixteen, word came from Honolulu that Mr. McTavish, the HBC agent there, wished a transfer. Capt. McNeill was assigned to the post. And he took Lucy with him to Hawaii to help find a suitable house for the family.

She loved the sunshine and the flowers and the smiles of the friendly natives. And maybe it was her enthusiasm that made Mr. McTavish think twice about leaving a post that was a very choice one indeed. In any case, he decided to stay. And the McNeills sailed home.

Victoria was now the capital of the new Crown Colony of Vancouver Island. And her brief stay there provided a wonderful time for the colonial young lady, although the Staines's school had collapsed. For Hamilton Moffatt, a handsome eighteen-year-old Irish gentleman, had arrived as a Company clerk. And the two fell in love. But all too soon, her father took her back to Fort Rupert.

Then, by wonderful chance—or by arrangement? —Mr. Moffatt was posted to Fort Rupert. But there was trouble at Fort Rupert. The California Gold

Rush was luring the coal miners away from the Company; and the Company was holding them to their contracts. There were riots. There were desertions. There were murders. And Lucy's brother-in-law, young Mr. Blenkinsop, had to keep the place going while Capt. McNeill was at sea. He and Hamilton went out on dangerous missions, while the girls waited in anguish.

Then, just before Christmas, Mrs. McNeill died. Some of the children were packed off to school in England. And Lucy went north with her father to his new posting at Fort Simpson, leaving Hamilton to the gloom and dangers of a bad posting.

Soon her father set tongues wagging all along the coast. He fell in love again, this time with the handsome daughter of a Nishga chief. But there were complications. The lady was already one of the wives of old Sakau'wan (Sharp Teeth), head chief of an Eagle Clan.

By native custom, a wife could leave her husband by making certain ceremonial arrangements, which the high-ranking Wolf lady did. But pride and humiliation were mighty forces among the native peoples of the Northwest Coast. And Sharp Teeth was deeply humiliated by his young wife's desertion.

To publicly wipe out his shame, he gathered mountains of gifts and mountains of food for a magnificent potlatch. He invited the neighboring chiefs to the feast to witness his ridiculing of the fickle lady. And at the potlatch, he sang a song full of scathing for the Flighty One; he showed the "poor beaver skins" he was sending to her. The "poor beaver skins" were gorgeous, matched marten pelts that she—to her shame!—would not be able to return in kind.

And now her humiliation was not to be borne. The only way to wipe out her shame was to send Sharp Teeth a gift more valuable than the gift he had sent.

Lucy understood that her father could not ignore this public ridiculing of his wife; his prestige along the coast was at stake as well as hers. So the girl encouraged her father to secretly arrange for the purchase of a magnificent Haida canoe decorated with his wife's Wolf totem. And this they sent, very publicly, to Sharp Teeth.

Now the shame was once more on the other side. The Flighty One had bettered Sharp Teeth's gift. So, to wipe out his new shame, he planned another, even more splendid potlatch. And at the potlatch, he sang an even more scathing song.

The captain's lady seethed. Again she must wipe out her shame or be humiliated along the North Coast.

She shared leadership of her Wolf Clan with a brother. And now the brother died. So she decided to raise a memorial totem pole to him; and at the ceremonial raising of the pole, she would publicly assume leadership of the Clan.

Capt. McNeill willingly paid Oyai, the greatest carver in the area, to carve the pole. He willingly paid for the mountains of gifts and the mountains of food for the guest-witnesses at the potlatch. And he willingly took his wife back to her old village for the ceremony. Lucy went with them.

When the pole had been raised, his wife stood beside it while her Speaker told the legends of the proud hereditary crests it carried. Then she claimed the Chief's name, Niskinawelk. The claim was publicly validated by the guests. And now, Mrs. McNeill was as high among the Wolves as Sharp Teeth was among the Eagles. He could do nothing more to her. She could go back home with her head high.

Lucy's own romance had to wait on time and postings. But, at long last, the McNeills went back to Victoria. Lucy sent to Honolulu for a tucked and embroidered white muslin gown, a shirred satin bonnet, and a bridal veil.

The wedding was a gala affair, with one of the governor's daughters as a bridesmaid. The fort guns boomed, the bell rang, the dogs howled, men fired off muskets, fiddles and fifes and drums led the usual parade outside the palisades. And Lucy went off with her husband to Fort Kamloops, an interior post where great brigades of horses replaced the canoes and sailing ships and steamers of the Coast. As Chief Trader's wife, she was well supplied with servants. But as her father's daughter, she missed the sea.

Company life was a wandering one. And before she got back to the sea, there was another interior posting, to Fort St. James on Stuart Lake. This was the major depot for collecting furs of the northern interior. From here they were taken south by river boat to Fort Alexandria, where they were transferred to the horse brigades sent out from Fort Kamloops.

Here, there was an older man in charge, with four lively daughters and many "young gentlemen." So there was much dancing and merrymaking. But Lucy still longed for the sea. And after four years, she was happy to leave in a fur-lined cariole pulled across the snow and ice by dogs in bright harness a-jingle with sleigh bells. She was leaving the Company; for Hamilton was going into the Indian Agency at Victoria.

Her father was waiting for them in his new home, a home handsomely furnished through a sister in Boston.

But Lucy soon had her own home. And now, while she was still in her twenties, a lovely thing happened. One of Her Majesty Queen Victoria's survey ships' captains, Sir George Henry Richards, named the lovely little island with its brood of islets after the captain's daughter. The *Lucy Islands*.